Lock Down Publications and Ca$h
Presents

I0637442

THE PLUG'S RUTHLESS DAUGHTER 3

A FIGHT TO THE END

Tony Daniels

First Edition 2025

Printed in the United States of America

This is a work of fiction. Names, characters, places, and incidents either are products of the author's imagination or are used fictitiously. Any similarity to actual events or locales or persons, living or dead, is entirely coincidental.

Lock Down Publications
P.O. Box 944
Stockbridge, GA 30281
www.lockdownpublications.com

Like our page on Facebook: Lock Down Publications
www.facebook.com/lockdownpublications.ldp

Stay Connected with Us!

Text **LOCKDOWN** to 22828 to stay up-to-date with new releases, sneak peaks, contests and more…

Like our page on Facebook:
Lock Down Publications

Join Lock Down Publications/The New Era Reading Group

Visit our website:
www.lockdownpublications.com

Follow us on Instagram:
Lock Down Publications

Email Us: We want to hear from you!

Acknowledgements

All Praises are due to Allah! This book is dedicated to all my readers and for the ones that don't know me. It has been a rough road but thanks to God (Allah) and many family members who continued to push me to a write a book one more time and another one after that. Cash, you have given me a chance to show my talent, and I want to thank you for signing me because Lock Down Publications is an excellent company. I appreciate all the wisdom you have given me. It means more to me now than ever. Now, I truly understand struggle and putting my all in to be a better writer. My mission is to make sure none of it was in vain. I'm standing on everything you taught me, and despite the many obstacles I face because of our bond, my love and loyalty is unwavering.

It means more to me… now to my homies locked down in Yuzou Mississippi Federal Prison, this book is for you. Rambo, LA, Dee, Mas. Mill, Lil One, and all my Muslim brothers. To all names I didn't mention, to you also. Once again, a special shoutout to Mrs. Mills for giving me the tools, and courage, to be a better man in society. You have taught me how to turn good into greatness. You always kept a smile on your face and treat everyone with great respect.

I just want to say thank you, Clay Mills, for being a real teacher that never beat around the brush about anything. Shoutout to my little brother Michael Jones, better known as Dirty Mike, man this long journey almost over with. Last but not least, to all my homies that got caught up in the 2015 Blind Justice operation and yes, we are about to come to a dead road and be free soon.

Hold your head up high, Jesse Williams, better known as "Loc." Rambo, man, you have taught me more than a little bit and each day it's an honor to be able to talk to you about life and how to be successful. Rambo, you're a true friend and I want to do a book with you soon. Shoutout to "Thug Town." Blytheville, Arkansas, we on the map.

Dedications

To my nephew, Ray Ray. Man, there's not a day uncle doesn't think about you in prison. Many times, I wish I could come visit you and just share a few words of wisdom, and I promise once I touch down, I will hold you down. Keep your head up in there. Uncle Tubb loves you, Ray Ray. This book is dedicated, soldier for life.

Chapter 1

"Uh fuck! Oh shit." Mimi rolled her beautiful eyes in annoyance as she faked pleasure. Chuck put her in different positions, from the buck to doggy style, and with each power stroke, she lurched forward. Mimi had gone to go holler at the young nigga wearing a little bit of nothing to entice him into purchasing her pussy. Her proposition was as simple as ABC. "Give me some dope and I'll give you some ass." Needless to say, Chuck's thirsty ass was sold without a sales pitch. All he could think about was running up in the woman that was old enough to be his grandmother.

The young nigga took her around the corner to his grandfather's house, since he wouldn't be home, on account that he was at a toke game at his homie's crib. As soon as he had gotten Mimi behind closed doors, he was stripping down and trying to slide up in her raw dog.

She had to slow his roll because she wasn't going for that. The way she saw it, if he was so eager to raw dick a bitch he didn't know from a can of paint, and there wasn't any telling how many other nasty bitches he'd slung his big dick to without strapping up. Even after he offered to throw her a half of sixteen for the experience, she still declined. He had this lustful look in his eyes, and she thought that he might try to just take the pussy. Fearing so, she carefully sharpened the blade cutter she'd brought along within arm's reach, just in case he was got on some rape shit.

After several failed attempts at trying to get Mimi to let him smash without a rubber, Chuck finally gave up and slid on a condom. Now, although safe sex wasn't nearly good as bare backing a bitch, he was wearing a thin latex condom so he could still feel a little something-something.

Chuck stood behind Mimi, with her bodacious ass cheeks spread apart. His long fingers were buried into her meaty buttocks as he watched his dick pump in and out of her hot, gooey pussy. Sweat trickled from his face and splashed upon the slit of her slightly hairy ass crack. The veins bulged in his forehead and thick neck. He gritted and licked his big lips, feeling his nut suck swell and the mushroom tip of his dick throb.

Bam! Bam! Bam!

His pelvis collided with her rear as he deposited and withdrew his hardness. "Yeah, fuckin bitch, you like that, huh? You like how a young thug nigga get off in them muthafuckin' guts, huh? Huh?"

"Ooh, yes, big daddy… fuck me! Fuck me, harder! Faster, harder, oh, yes!" she called out with her eyes rolled to their whites. He had her long hair pulled back and the bottom of her chin was exposed. She jolted back and forth as he pummeled her from behind, the sound of their wet skin smacking against each other bounced off the walls, inside of the living room.

Bam! Bam! Bam!

Chuck smacked Mimi across her dampened ass cheeks viciously and caused her to cry in pain. Smacking her buttocks, he left red hand imprints behind like his palms had been painted or some shit. Releasing her hair, Chuck held his hands behind his back and ordered her to throw her ass back into him. He watched excitedly and licked his lips, seeing her booty mash up against his pelvis, and then bounce back into form repeatedly.

"Faster, bitch, throw that ass in a circle!" Smack! He smacked her ass again and she threw herself into him faster.

This caused the slapping sound that their skin made while meeting to grow louder and louder. Before he knew it, he was about to explode, so he grabbed her aggressively by her hips to stop her while she was in motion.

"Stay right there, babe, don't move!" Chuck ordered. He pulled off his rubber and stroked his dick back and forth. His creamy white jizz oozed out of the head of his dick and splattered in droplets on Mimi's ass, sliding between the crack of her thick ass. Wiping the sweat from his forehand, he took a long deep breath and looked down at that bodacious ass of hers. He smiled, showing his shiny diamond grill, which twinkled. He licked his top lip and smacked his conquest on her supple behind, sending a ripple through her thick ass.

Afterwards, he hopped out of bed and walked towards the bathroom, holding the nut-filled rubber pinched between his fingers. He shut the door halfway and opened the lid of the commode, dropping the used rubber inside the toilet. He threw his head back and shut his eyelids, whizzing inside the bowl and relieving his bladder. He farted, and his nose scrunched up, that's when he looked down and flushed the toilet.

I gotta take a power shit." Still holding his dick in his hand, Chuck kicked the bathroom door shut and plopped down on the commode. As soon as Mimi saw this, she sifted through the pockets of his jeans until she came up with a bundle of drug money. It was mostly singles but she didn't give a damn. It was more than what she had, which was nothing. Having hit what she believed was the lottery, she recovered the sandwich bag of white crack rocks stashed beneath the cushion of the bed they were fucking on. Holding up the sandwich bag, she smiled at it in delight. She then wiped the nut off her ass with a Nike shirt that Chuck had left behind and tossed it aside.

Hastily, she pulled up her skirt and stashed the bag inside her secret pocket. Next, she reached over the bed and picked up her trick's .380 from the floor. She heard Chuck breaking wind as he went about the task of taking a shit, the sound resonating from the bathroom.

Mimi pushed open the window and flung the handgun out, sending it hurtling across the way into the yard of the neighboring house. Hearing the toilet being flushed startled her and she dashed across the bedroom, hearing the door squealing as it opened. Chuck's eyes stretched wide open, and his mouth formed an O, not believing his eyes. The middle-aged woman looked like a blur flying across his line of vision. His eyes darted to the couch, and he noticed that a cushion was missing, and his gun had also been taken. Furious, he took off behind Mimi, who just threw open the door, flying out of the house and hurrying down the steps.

Chuck grabbed a firewood poker out of the living room and chased her. He was about ten feet away life and occasionally glanced. I over her shoulder, eyes fill with fright and mouth hanging open. Her face was shiny from sweet and she was breathing huskily, breasts rising and falling with each breath from her in the middle of the street.

"Bitch, I'm killing you!" Chuck called out as he ran behind her, gripping the firewood poker with both of his hands. He clutched it so tight that veins bulged in his hands. When he finally caught up to her, he was going to crack open her fucking brain.

The occasional car passing through the street would slow down to see what was going on between the two of them, but then they would keep on going. Chuck lifted the firewood poker above his head, seeing that he was closing the distance between him and Mimi. He was crossing into the intersection when blinking lights came from his left. By the time he whipped around, he was overwhelmed by the brightness of an approaching vehicle's headlights. His eyelids stretched wide open and his mouth formed an O.

Boom!

Chuck went over the hood of the approaching car and scattered across its rooftop. He bounced off the trunk of the car and landed on his side wincing, firewood poker clanging to the ground. The vehicle's driver's door opened and on older black man hopped out, running to the back of his automobile. Concern was plastered across his face as he took a closer look at Chuck. He was still breathing. Feeling someone at his back, he turned around, and the bitch that was approaching at the rear froze in her tracks. She looked afraid and didn't know what to do.

"Argh, fuck, my back! I broke my back!" Chuck squeezed his eyelids shut and gritted his teeth, turning his head from side to side. He tightened his jaws repeatedly, causing the veins at his temple and big forehead to throb. He was in great pain and couldn't move, and he was pretty sure that he was paralyzed from the neck down.

Mustafa, the man that had hit Chuck, heard him complaining of his pain, but he didn't even bother to address him. The woman that seemed to be frozen stiff had his undivided attention. Mustafa's brows furrowed as he stared at the woman. He wasn't sure if she was Mimi, but she sure as hell resembled her. He had to be sure that it was her before he got at her though. He didn't want an innocent lie on his conscience.

Taking this into consideration, Mustafa pulled out the folded-up photograph that he'd taken from Mimi's apartment. Quickly, he unfolded the photograph and looked at it. He looked back and forth between the photo and the woman, that's when it dawned on him that the lady standing before him and the one in the photo was indeed one and the same.

"Mimi?" Mustafa called out to her to see if she would answer.

Hesitantly, Mimi, responded to him. "What's up? Do I know you?"

11

Instantly, Mustafa dropped the photo and swiftly drew his .40 Glock from the small of his back. Seeing him going for what she believed was a handgun, Mimi's eyelids stretched wide open and her heart beat harder inside of her chest. Realizing that she was in immediate danger, she took off running in the opposite direction.

"Bitch! Bitch! Bitch!" Mustafa sounded off angrily and opened fire on her as she retreated with her life. "Bitch!" he cursed when he realized that Mimi had gotten out of his firing range distance. Hurriedly, he ran over to his vehicle and hopped behind the wheel. He threw that bitch in reverse and floored the pedal. The automobile went flying backwards until its driver whipped it back in the intersection of the conjoining residential streets. He then threw his car into drive and floored the gas pedal to the floor, flying down the street, trying to catch up with Mimi. Seeing her coming up ahead, he got a grip on his black .40 Glock handgun and looked out of the driver's side window. Coming up on his target rather quickly, he pointed his gun out of the window and shot at her. Mimi hollered out in terror, but she wasn't hit. She ducked down low, holding her arms over her head and running for her life. Seeing that she was getting away, Mustafa bucked his whip up and took off after her. This bitch was fast as hell.

"You can run, bitch, but I will find you! That's for damn sure because I'm getting that ass, bitch! You hear me, hoe? I said, I'ma get that ass, bitch, once again!" Mustafa said aloud several times as if she could hear him from the distance she was. Gripping the steering wheel with one hand, he used the other to reload his Glock .40 handgun. If he didn't do anything else that night, he was going to kill Mimi's nasty ass.

***

THE PLUG'S RUTHLESS DAUGHTER 3 | TONY DANIELS

Boss Chick and Con were looking all around as they cruised through the block on their Range Rover. Something ahead got Con's attention. He saw someone hauling ass in his direction with a car following beside them. The driver was hanging outside the window, blazing bullets after bullet at the person running, trying to lay them down. Con didn't know what it was, but something told him that they should follow the car that was chasing after whomever it was running.

"Babe, babe, follow that car," Con told Boss Chick as he checked the magazine inside his gun.

"What, are you crazy?" Boss Chick frowned up at him.

"You know a nigga crazy, babe. Now follow that car." He smacked the magazine back into the bottom of his gun and chambered a live round inside its head. He then impatiently tapped his weapon against his thighs as Boss Chick went flying down the block after the car that was pursuing the person on foot.

Boom! Boom!

***

Mustafa pulled his car up on the sidewalk and knocked over several trash cans, spilling their contents. He was just in time to see Mimi hauling ass past him. Grabbing his gun, he threw open his door in a hurry and jumped out on the sidewalk. Seeing Mimi running as fast as she could towards a shabby looking house, he took off running after her. Heart pounding, adrenaline pumping, Mimi darted into the yard of the shabby looking house and up the steps. She frantically looked over her shoulder and pounded on the door.

The impacts from her pounding caused paint chips to fall from the old peeling door. As soon as the door of the shooting gallery was pulled open, she barged her way inside. The door slammed into the bitch that opened it, and she bumped her head against the wall. Scowling, she looked her way and called her a crackhead bitch, when she went to slam the door. Shit, Mustafa came charging up the steps, gun pointed.

Old girl that had opened the door, went to lift her Tec-9 to open fire, but the woman that belonged to True Light Church, Sister Mary, sent one through her forehead, but it blew a large chunk out of the back of her brains. Blood and brain fragments splattered against the wall, and she collapsed where she stood. Mustafa and Sister Mary ran away from the house. Sister Mary's adrenaline was jacked and murdering Mimi was her sole focus, so she didn't smell the overwhelming odors of feces, urine and vomit consuming the place.

Chapter 2

The bathroom door opened, and Karla stepped out wearing tight pink Victoria's Secret bikini cut panties that were all up in her pussy lips. From where she stood, Rambo could see a bald golden sex lip on each side of her crotch band. She also had on a small tank top that stopped just below her titties. Both of her nipples poked through the material.

She rubbed the front of her panties and ran her tongue across her lips. "You acted like you was gon' tear your dude's head off over me. Do you have any idea how that made me feel?" she asked as she walked over to Rambo and stood between his legs.

Rambo rubbed all over her thick ass cheeks. Rambo squeezed them and smacked them just enough to make them jiggle. "When have I ever played games about you, babe? You remember when we were kids? I knocked your so-called nigga out for calling you a hoe. You know what it is." Rambo spread her ass cheeks and ran his finger up and down her crease, feeling the string that was all up in her ass.

Karla laughed and placed her hands on his big shoulders, leaning down and kissing his lips. "I remember his whole crew jumped on you, and then later that day you shot his ass. You ain't been back in Chicago since then." She licked her lips, then sucked them into her mouth, moaning passionately like a freaky bitch.

Rambo kissed Karla back hard, then broke it. "Turn around and back up. Let me eat that pussy and that ass from the back." Rambo felt like he needed to taste Karla bad. For some reason, seeing all of them chasing her all day had Rambo feeling some type of way." He licked her pretty stomach and turned her around.

Karla bent over and backed into his face. His nose went right up her ass crack. He yanked her panties to the side and licked her slit, holding her hips before going to work like he was starving for that forbidden body.

She reached behind herself and pulled her ass cheeks apart. "Umm… yes, eat me, Rambo. Unn, just like you used to when we were kids and played hide and seek. Unnn, you remember that, nigga?"

He pinched her clit and drove his tongue in and out of her back door before sucking on her clit and licking her slit. Up and down, side to side, he kept going with her ass cheeks on his face.

She reached under herself and played with her pussy. "Rambo... I want you to fuck me so bad, baby. Unn! I need you to fuck a bitch, please. Please give me some dick. nice and hard. I'm begging you. young nigga!" she screamed.

Rambo was sucking all over her ass cheeks by this point, while playing with her clitoris, pinching it, sending chills through her soft body.

"Unn-unn, baby! Please help me! Yes!" She spread her legs wider apart. Rambo turned his head sideways, trapping both of her pussy lips, then ran his tongue in and out of her. "Fuck this shit, Rambo. Fuck this! I want some dick, nigga." She stood up and laid in the bed on her back, pulling her panties to the side and rubbing her pussy in crazy circles. "Let me see your big dick, baby, before you fuck me. Let me see you stroke it like when we were young kids, and I was scared of it. I just wanna be a young woman again." She arched her back and slid three fingers into herself. "Oh shit, please, let a bitch see that dick."

Rambo dropped his pants and boxers, then stood before her with his dick rock hard. He looked between Karla's legs and saw how fat her bald pussy was, with the way its lips opened to reveal her pink insides and saw the juice coming out of her hole. He couldn't help stroking his dick. "Unn, I'm finna murder this pussy, Karla. You know it, too," he said, watching her finger herself faster and harder while her eyes stayed pinned on his dick.

Karla took her fingers and opened her lips real wide, then smashed them together while her fingers on her right hand shot in and out of her. Her thumb assaulted her clit in mad circles. "Unn, unn. You gon' fuck me like when we were young kids? Huh, Rambo?" She raised her ass from the bed and opened her thick thighs wider. Her toes curled before she straightened them all over again, and still her eyes never left the sights of his dick. Rambo could tell that she wanted it bad.

Rambo got on the bed right between her thick legs, leaned down and licked all over her pussy coated fingers, sucking on her wrist while she continued to dig deep within her pussy. Tasting her saltiness, he loved it. "I want this pussy, Karla. I'm gone murder this pussy. I promise you that, baby." He yanked her hand out of the way and sucked her clit into his mouth again, nipping at it with his teeth, while she reached under him and took ahold of his dick, pulling on it like a lollipop.

"Mmmm-a! I want this dick, babe. Please give it to me, now!" she whimpered, opening her thighs, allowing for him to swallow her running cum juice. She was all over his lips and chin. He could taste her heavily on his long tongue.

Rambo stood on his knees and pushed Karla down to the bed, sucking and biting on her neck hard while she moaned in her ear and tried to pull him on top of her. Rambo wiggled out of her embrace and tore her panties from her frame, then pulled her shirt up to expose her pretty titties with the huge nipples. Squeezing her breasts together, he sucked the right nipple first and then the left nipple, pulling on them with his mouth.

"Ahh! Shit! Please, hurry! Fuck me, nigga, I can't take it no more. I need this dick," she said, reaching between them and trying to force his dick into her little tight hole.

Every time the big head went into the crease, he turned his hips to make it fall back out. He knew the more he teased her, the wetter she would become. He thought about all the games they played when they were young. She'd always hide in a spot that she knew a nigga could find her, and once he did, he'd pull up her little church skirt and lay it on her back, get between her legs and hump like a dog into her center while she held his waist. It was how it all started. Now she was a woman, fine and thick as hell, ready to go. He couldn't wait to be inside of her body.

She sat up and kissed all over his lips, licking them and leaning into his face. "Do me, baby. Please, I wanna feel you inside of me right now. I'm begging you." She lay on her back again, spreading her legs wide. Pussy juices ran out of her lips and oozed down her thick ass cheeks. Her scent was heavy in the room and intoxicating him on so many levels.

"Alright, I'm finna fuck this fat pussy on some grown player shit then. Let's get it."

Rambo picked up her thick left thigh, put it up against his chest while he placed his dick head on her pussy hole. and rubbed it up and down her wet slit, before ramming inside. Bam! Bam!

"Uhhn! Shit! Fuck yeah! Fuck a bitch's brains out!" she screamed, already shaking with her pussy walls vibrating.

His hips slammed into her again and again, harder, faster, bam, bam! The bed rocked back and forth, making all kinds of loud sounds. He leaned down and sucked all over her neck, licking up the hot sweat there while she moaned at the top of her lungs.

"Un, un, un! Shit yes, daddy! Rambo, you're fucking me so hard." She arched her back and started to shake all over again, this shit was crazy.

Her pussy was skeeting its juices all over his dick while she bit his lips and rubbed all over his ass, pulling him into her so he could fuck her deeper and harder. Her center felt like a hot, silky furnace. Forbidden, taboo, and right up his alley. He'd been lusting after her ever since they were young. Now he was knee deep within that forbidden pussy and loving every power stroke was of it.

They tongue kissed loudly, moaning into each other's faces while his dick drove in and out of her pussy. Using both of her arms for leverage, he was digging as deep as he could into her body while her eyes rolled into the back of her head and she held her mouth wide open in an O shape.

"Cum in me, Rambo. Let me feel the hotness." Once again, she arched her back while he pounded her out and sped up the pace.

Now he was going so fast that it sounded like the bed was trying to come through the wall. The springs were so loud that it seemed like they were jumping up and down in the bed like little kids, instead of fucking like they were.

His eyes rolled into the back of his head, then he looked down again and saw how his twelve-inch dick was going in and out her pussy. Every time he rammed forward, her sex lips would smash together, and when he pulled backward, they would open up widely and leave his dick coated in her cream. He started to think about who she was and their relationship to each other, and it was too much for him to handle. He folded her into a ball, slamming his dick into her. He got about five more long strokes in before he was coming deep within her channel, feeling her long nails scratch all over his lower back, but it didn't stop him from plunging forward harder and harder while his cum shot into her pussy.

"Uhhh! Uhhh! I feel it. Ummm, yes sir," were her last words before they spent the next ten minutes kissing and sucking all over each other's bodies. They couldn't get enough.

She broke our embrace, took his dick and sucked him into her mouth, licking her juices from it loudly. "We taste good together." More sucking. "Umm, we taste so good together." She licked up and down it while he rubbed and squeezed her round ass.

He wanted to hit that muhfucka, and he knew that before she went back to Chicago he would. He didn't give a fuck what took place. *Now she is in Arkansas getting fucked by a country boy. I had to beat that pussy up for the city.*

She sucked him for another six minutes, then climbed up his body, took his hard dick and slid it back inside her. "Umm, baby." Then she laid her head on his chest, riding him real nice and slow.

He gripped that fat ass booty with both hands, one on each cheek, guiding her up and down his dick. "I love this pussy, Karla. You hear a nigga talking to you? I love this shit," he said, rubbing into her ass crack.

She sat up and looked down on him, with both of her breasts jiggling. "Mmm, it's yours, Rambo. It's always been yours. You just never came back to the Chi. Unn, this large dick. I missed you. I swear, I missed you so much." She laid her head back on to his chest, licking his nipple before hugging him and stopping her ride on his dick. "Can you hold me for the rest of the night? I really need to be held by you." She disconnected their sexes and laid on her side, pulling his arm around her.

They spooned and he kissed the back of her neck. He loved doing that to a beautiful female when he held them, especially after fucking because all of their scent wafted from their scalps and went right up to his nostrils. There was nothing like the scent of a woman so beautiful and soft. It was a nigga's weakness.

Rambo kissed her neck and held her more firmly. "I ain't got to leave and go back down there. I'd make sure you're good if you stayed down here with me in Arkansas. That's my word." He kissed her again and humped her ass.

She pushed backward and exhaled loudly. "I'd love to stay down here with you, Rambo, but you got a lot going on. You barely have any time for me right now. What would you do if I did stay? What about your family? I already want you to myself." She laughed and laid her head backward.

Rambo reached around and cuffed her left breast, running his thumb across her erect nipple. Like he said, if she stayed down here with him, he'd make sure she was good. "Take that how you want to. Ain't nothing like this forbidden boy right here. You know how we get down."

Karla rubbed her ass in Rambo's lap and giggled. "Yeah, I guess you right, because when you were in this pussy, all I kept thinking about is who you are, and it got me wetter than the Mississippi River. I know, I got problems." She raised her legs as she felt him searching with his large dick head for her hole again.

Rambo slid easily into her hole and slammed forward. "Yeah, you and me both, baby."

Chapter 3

Bam! Bam! Bam! The AR-15 jumped, in her, found their target again and again. Her bullets slammed into Gucci's chest and knocked him backward, causing him to fall onto the hood of his red Lexus truck. Bambi opened the door and started shooting the truck up. Her bullets flew into the windshield, shattering it, while the other bullets implanted themselves in the truck exterior. One of the niggas jumped behind the wheel like a fool and got wet up several times in the head and chest. He crashed the truck into a car full of bitches. Bambi could hear hoes screaming at the top of their lungs. Bambi jumped back with her car and threw it in drive, leaving the scene at a fast speed.

The alley had about ten stray dogs inside of it. Bambi and Fresh jumped out of the car as a big truck pulled up. The alley lights had been shot out, and it was so dark that the day's eyes were different shades of electric blue.

Bambi slammed the barrel of her gun to Fresh's temple and pulled the trigger, blowing his brains against the driver's side door. His body fell against the door and he hit the ground. The dogs took off running in every direction. Bambi reached across him and opened the driver's door and pushed his body out the way. She jumped back out and reached inside his pockets, turning them inside out, trying her best to make it look like a drug deal went bad.

Then, Bambi stood up and looked down on Fresh with her gun extended. "Fuck nigga! Bitch ass nigga!" Boom! Boom!

Boom! The fire from her gun lit up the alley again and again. Bambi ran back to the car and removed the duffle bags, threw them on her shoulders after wiping down the inside of her car and broke down the alley, running at full speed.

Bambi was running toward the local store and it started pouring rain, just as lightning flashed across the sky, thunder rumbled. She didn't make it too far before shit hit the fan. She looked down the block, just as the side door to the purple truck's side door opened, and several goons jumped from the back armed with black ski masks over their faces and assault rifles in their hands. Boom! Boom! Boom! Their bullets slammed into the local corner store right beside her, knocking out glass which shattered on the ground, and causing sparks to fly into the air.

"Fuck! Shit!" she said and ran into the store like a damn fool as more and more bullets were popped in her direction.

Bambi ducked behind the counter, pulled her .40 Glock out of her waist and busted out the side window with two shots. Everyone in the store ran for cover. Some screamed and begged for the Lord to save them. It sounded like utter chaos until the truck screeched its way down the block and disappeared. Bambi ran and opened the front door, running back outside into the rain, bussing her gun at the truck.

The store owner lay with his back up against the wall, holding his chest. Blood leaked through his fingers as he winced in pain with the rain beating down on his dark face. The store owner handed Bambi his keys and they jumped into his Benz truck down the block.

"Come on, I'm in pain, take me to the hospital," the store owner screamed out in pain.

"Fuck that shit! I'm on the run for more shit and you can let me out right here and drive yourself." She stopped the vehicle and got in the middle of the hood.

"Please! Please!" The man took his last breath standing and fell to the ground, shaking in pain. Five minutes later, he died right beside the Benz, as Bambi continued to run to her nearest friend's house.

***

Boss Chick and Con noticed two cars creeping up slowly without their lights on, and they knew it was them. Boss Chick was the first person to start letting off shots.

Boom! Boom! Boom!

She let her Glock with the extended clip go with precision.

Boom! Boom! Boom!

Con let the AR-15 loose.

The cars stopped and four men jumped out, letting shots ring back. They were inside Tubb's Corner lot store on Main Street. That's why Arie's crew picked that area, because they never thought Boss Chick and Con would catch them slipping.

Boss Chick and Con were lighting up the block as each crew member tried to badly injure one of the other crew. Cross tried to run behind a wall and caught a bullet in the leg. Con fired in that direction to give Boss Chick a chance for cover. Police sirens were heard in the distance and were getting closer.

Boss Chick shot Cross in the chest three times, dropping him immediately!

They ran for their car, shooting wildly in Con and Boss Chick's direction, but missing everything. As Aries' crew got into their car, the back window exploded, causing shattered glass to fly everywhere. A piece hit an old man in his right eye. He grabbed at his eyes as blood leaked out.

"Get us the fuck outta here, Boss Chick," he said, pulling out of the parking lot and heading toward the crib.

When they arrived, the trap spot was empty, so they drove to Boss Chick's mansion for the night. When they walked in, it felt like all the blood in his body drained out. "Money over everything, nigga!" Boss Chick yelled out loud to him.

Boss Chick and Con had the black duffle bags in their presence that Arie's crew had dropped running for cover. They didn't even have to open it up to see what it was. Con went into the closet and opened one of the duffle bags and put everything in it. "I thought it was five million dollars in cash by the thousand bands stacks in rubber bands." He was happy as hell. "Hey babe, we are straight for a minute."

"Why you say that?"

"We have about five-million dollars profit for free."

"Damn, we straight. Let's go, babe." They walked out the front door to their car. Boss Chuck didn't want Con to think she needed him, so she wanted to get her half, and they go their separate ways. She decided to walk back into the house to get something upstairs for her sister Maria on the east side for her birthday. She arrived upstairs and heard some strange sounds.

"Damn, baby. Don't stop!" Karla begged breathlessly, opening her legs in order to give Rambo more access to her love tunnel.

She hadn't been sure it was possible, but she was able to place her legs all the way back, touching her ears as Rambo practically pushed his entire face inside her pussy lips. The way he was sucking on her clit almost made her cum instantly. His tongue game was on point, and Karla was speechless at the moment. There was nothing in the world that could keep her quiet with the way Rambo could with his tongue licking, sucking, and flicking through the folds of her pussy.

"Mmmm!" Rambo hummed into her dripping wet pussy, tasting the strawberry flower coming from it.

Rambo's head game caused so much pleasure that Karla almost felt dizzy. She closed her eyes tight as he started lightly kissing her up and down her swollen clit. Every time he pushed his face into it, it made a sucking noise when he pulled away. Karla couldn't take it anymore. She needed some good dick, and she wanted more now.

"Baby, please!" she mumbled, with her eyes closed, holding his head. "I want to feel you inside me now!"

She felt Rambo pull back before sticking three fingers inside of her pussy. Then she felt his warm mouth over her left breast, sucking on it while he squeezed the other with his free hand. She almost screamed out loud, but she didn't want to wake anybody up in the house. Karla didn't know Boss Chick was standing at the bedroom door. Karla started jerking badly, and although she didn't want to, she was about to cum.

"Not yet, shit!" he hollered out. "You better not do it until I say so, baby!"

He pulled his fingers out and removed his mouth from her breast. Kayla opened her eyes and caught a glimpse of him right before his dick entered her pussy, pushing her walls open even wider than she was ready to go at that moment.

The first thing that came to her mind was to meet every thrust, but she was no match for a real player with a big dick. He was tearing that shit up, she loved the way a down south nigga put it down.

"Oh shit, baby, I can't take it anymore. Shit! Yeah, tear this pussy up, country boy!" she moaned loudly, "Rambo, you the best, baby."

Rambo's phone started blowing up. He and Karla both groaned at the sound. She stopped moving her body so he could get up.

"Fuck! I thought I had it on silent, baby!" he said. "I'm not going to answer it yet. Whoever it is can wait."

Rambo began pounding away again at her pussy like he was in a rush to bust his nut. Karla wrapped her legs around his waist and gave it back. They were in sync with their movements. She smiled in pleasure at the fact that he was putting her needs over his business affairs. The phone started ringing again.

"Agghhh!" Karla laughed. "Just go ahead and answer it because it's killing my vibe."

Rambo grabbed his phone and shook his head as soon as he saw the screen. He didn't need to talk to them right now, they were about their business, so he could speak with them later about the issue. When it rang once more, he figured something was up, so he answered.

"What's up?" he said, walking out the bedroom and out of earshot of Karla so she couldn't hear his conversation.

We had a problem, bro," Boss Chick responded, speaking in code just in case their phones were tapped.

"Where you at now?"

"Outside the bedroom. Listening to you fuck a bitch!"

"Okay. Go to your trap spot and wait for me."

"I'm my way now." Rambo was not being told the truth at the moment. He wanted to know what had happened. He went back into the room and got dressed. Karla could tell something was wrong by the look on his face. She didn't press the issue though, because no matter what, she supported her men. After getting dressed, Rambo gave Karla a kiss and rushed out the front door. When he got into his car, he checked his clip to make sure it was fully loaded. He just wanted to be prepared for whatever happened.

***

A few minutes later, he was parking outside of Boss Chick's crib. As soon as he walked in, Boss Chick and Con were sitting on the couch with blank expressions on their faces. There was a lot of tension in the house, so Con spoke first to try to ease it before Rambo got the news. "We have several Arie's men on smash now, fam. Everyone is buying dope from us, and if they're not, I'm sure I don't have to finish that statement," he said, giving Rambo a smile.

"That's cool and all, but I know you didn't call me all the way over here to tell me that, so what is it?" Rambo asked, looking at Boss Chick.

"We had a problem with getting the whereabouts of that nigga Aries, and we ended up killing his crew members!"

"Shit happens. He became a war. Did you at least get that nigga?"

"Almost! But he got away before we could kill him."

"His crew was with him, and we only bodied several of them."

"We are going back through his hood tomorrow," Boss Chick mentioned.

"No! Go past there tonight, and if you need more help, let me know. I want them dead soon," Con said.

They looked at Rambo, waiting for a reaction. "Well, I have business to handle," he said as he walked toward the front door and out to his car and drove away.

Chapter 4

Brandi strolled down Franklin, relishing in her ghetto dreams, she noticed a nigga staring her down. She was used to niggas' mouths watering as they imagined how the inside of her pussy felt. When she reached the corner, she stood there, knowing that she was the shit around town. With her low-waist jeans perfectly accentuating the gap between her slightly curved legs and six-foot-one-inch hourglass figure, in complete awe.

One nigga got too close to her, the more appealing she became. Her butterscotch complexion glistened under the down south hot sun. The wind slightly blew through her black hair, which stopped around midback. Her strawberry-glossed lips added more beautiful moments to her looks. She was sure the nigga felt he was supposed to have spotted her in print in South Carolina on a beach, instead of strolling down Franklin Street.

She paused for a moment and ogled the strange nigga up and down. She then folded her arms and smacked her lips before speaking. "Nigga, I'm not your baby. Save that lame ass shot for the next bitch, nigga."

"Hold up a minute," he said as he reached to grab her arm. She instantly pulled away with her eyes speaking for the nigga. He knew they read, *back the fuck off, nigga.* "I'm sorry, I didn't mean to grab on you like that, but I didn't want you to walk away."

"Hum huh," she said, rolling her sexy eyes to let the nigga know he was getting in her way.

"No disrespect, baby girl, but you are far too beautiful to be speaking with so much anger."

"Excuse me, nigga. Who the fuck you supposed to be around here? The dope man's son?"

"Nah, my dad is in the federal prison serving time for a drug charge he caught in 2015, and the feds gave him too much time for a methamphetamine charge," he said as tears fell from his eyes.

"So why how I speak matter to you, since you ain't no help," she said, hoping the nigga would keep walking.

"A nigga don't see a nigga with you or a diamond ring on your finger. I believe a chance at your heart can happen in the future."

"Maybe, nigga, I don't want a diamond ring or a nigga by my side. Feel me on that?"

"All beautiful queens deserve to be loved and blessed with the finest things in life, and you are definitely a beautiful queen."

"If you don't mind me asking, what's up with the police cars speeding up the street?"

She knew within seconds the street would be blocked off. Bambi liked having the gun, she'd murdered Fresh with, for her protection, and the other one was a backup for war with extra clips. She ran toward her friend's house and banged on her door until she opened it.

"Bitch, what's wrong with you?"

Bambi was breathing hard and couldn't speak clearly at the moment. "Here, take this." She took her Chanel backpack off her shoulders and handed it to her in tears. Her mouth dropped when she opened the backpack and saw all the money. "It's eighty thousand dollars to maintain yourself for a while until I get back."

"Damn, Bambi, you my best friend." Red placed a wet kiss on the side of Brandi's jaw. "Well, a bitch better get outta here fast." She'd never talked about the murder to Red and walked out of Red's house not knowing when she'd see her again. Bambi didn't give her money because she felt guilty about killing Fresh, but to buy her beauty shop that she always dreamed of having but never had the money. Bambi just wanted to make sure she was straight. Bambi made it down the block into the alley and dialed several friends' phone numbers, but nobody answered the phone. She reached to the side of her waist, grabbed her .380 handgun and put it to her head. As she had her finger on the trigger, she stated, I'm not going back to the feds or state anymore. I will handle all this shit in the street!"

Boom! Boom!

Several people ran to the alley to see where the loud sounds were coming from.

***

Karla zipped up the last duffle bag and dropped it on the floor beside the other duffle bag. Stepping before the dresser's mirror, she took one last pull from her blunt and put it down in the ashtray. Smoke rose from it and disappeared in the air. Picking up a beige rubber band, she stared at her reflection and pulled her long black hair into a ball with the black rubber band around it. Her eyelids had swollen from crying for so long and her pretty eyes were pink and glossy. Her thick cheeks on her face were soaking wet, having shed so many tears. Rambo had not been home since he'd left on a business trip to a small town in Arkansas called Dumas. She did everything in her power to keep Rambo and not go back to Chicago to be with him. Even if she failed, she couldn't sleep at night knowing that Rambo was not beside her at night.

Karla took another long puff from the blunt, pulling smoke into her lungs. She started to cough from inhaling the smoke. Allowing the smoke to roll around inside of her chest, she decided to blow the smoke back out. Afterwards, she finished the blunt and put the television on. She decided it was nothing -on, so she grabbed her duffle bags and headed for the front door. She made it outside to her car and opened the trunk and tossed the duffle bag in, slamming it shut. Now that was out of the way, she jumped behind the wheel of her 2025 Benz and peeled out of the parking lot. Her first stop was at the local corner store on Ash and Main. She pulled up to pump 3 and headed up to the bulletproof window to pay for the gas.

Karla's face frowned up when she saw the clerk grabbing the wrong bag of chips. "Nooo, them Cheetos hot," she stated and the woman gave her the correct chips. She was startled by the sudden bellow of a voice that caused her to drop the chips from her mouth.

"Bitch, gimme all your money. All of it, hoe! Now, goddamn it!" a masked person ordered. The person had sunken in, baggy eyes and pronounced cheekbones. He had on a dirty white Nike shirt and some dirty ass brown Timberland boots on. He looked around paranoid with the gun in his hand, as Karla moved slowly. The man worried that the laws might come soon. This was his first time making a move like this. This was the only way to get fast cash. Karla hurriedly searched through her purse trying to give the mean person the money in her pockets. He slapped her across the head with the gun. "Where the rest of the money?" his deep voice screamed out.

"It's in my trunk." She hit the keypad to pop it open. The man ran over to the trunk and reached in there and grabbed the duffle bag and snatched her purse, taking off running This nigga was faster than Carl Lewis.

A sad Karla looked at her hands and they were trembling uncontrollably. The robbery had her shaken up. As soon as the man left, she thought that her life was over. She reached under her seat and grabbed her 9mm handgun and put it in her mouth. "I cannot do this shit." She dropped the gun on the floor and drove off the parking lot. She grabbed her phone and called Rambo and finally got an answer. "Hello."

"What's up, baby?"

"I just got robbed and need you to come home, nigga, now!"

"Okay. I will be there. You be safe, get home now!"

"Alright, babe."

***

Boss Chick had been keeping a low profile. The last thing she wanted to do was to get extra because one of the fuck niggas stepped out of line, or because you do something crazy, Con like always. With all the cash Boss Chick had, it will set her up for a long period of time. Although a bitch still had trap spots in the hood, even got a mansion built in the center of West Rose and Maple Street on the west side. Standing outside on the porch, a group of niggas behind her trap spot exchanged money for days as she continued to look at the camera on her phone. All of a sudden, there were several cars driving by, drinking, music loud as many girls screamed out the window. A bitch was so caught up on the scene that she didn't hear the gunshots that were ringing in the air loud as fuck.

"Oh shit," Con screamed when he heard several shots. He had a clear view of Boss Chick running with an AR-15 she'd snatched off the couch on the front porch. She heard a loud explosion as the glass from the house's front window shattered. She ran to the car where Con was listening to music and pulled the latch back and forth. They were blasting out bullets like he had license to shoot. Boss Chick kept her head down in the car, as Con put the petal to the metal and sped off. But before he did, the nigga blasted off two last bullets, shattering the entire back window. Boss Chick was so scared, she farted. Con's nose filled up for a minute from the smell. Con looked down at her hands, and they were shaking. She was trying to remain calm as possible in a situation like this, but inside, she was freaking out in her mind. All it took was one bullet to end her like and that nigga who was chasing the car let out enough to kill them both.

Although her head was still down. She was given the second degree about what's going on. But she wasn't saying to much info before she got quiet again. Even with Boss Chick's head down, she was able to look to the side and see Con was sweating puddles. She stayed down for what seemed like another ten minutes until Con came to a stop.

"Boss Chick, I have to run in my house and get something. If you see anybody strange pull off and we'll meet up at your house, baby. Just drive far enough to get out of sight, then ditch the car and call a local cab to take you home." Boss Chick's hands were shaking, so she stuck them under her thighs because she didn't want Con to know how badly she was stressing at the moment. "Why can't you drop me off at home?"

Con lifted her chin and looked in her beautiful green eyes. "You my lady, I take care of you. You telling me you not my ride of die bitch?" he asked in the most serious voice she never heard before.

"Nigga, I got your back. Go handle what you have to do and if nobody shows up, then I'll be here waiting like you got twenty years in federal prison." She smiled.

When Con got out of the car, he just shook his head. He didn't know what type of bullshit Rambo was caught up in, but no nigga was worth dying for out here. It didn't matter now because in a blink of a second, Con was back with four big ass bags he put in the trunk of his car. There was dead silence as Con drove to his garage and pulled out his Benz.

She wanted to go home, but he begged her to stay with him at the hotel room he got. Without saying a word, he came up with a better master plan that will shock the world. He didn't want to run her away from him.

Con handed Boss Chick ten stacks, or what he called ten G's. She decided to stay with him at least for a minute, might not be all that bad. "What you think you would have done in this situation?"

Boss Chick hardly slept that whole night tossing and turning in the bed. Her stomach was growling because a hoe was starving for some soul food. She wanted to order something from Pizza Hut or some room service, but Con's paranoid ass didn't want anybody come to the room. Con went out and brought back some eggs and bacon from a local food store on the corner. Finally, her stomach was full as a tick, and she started asking Con questioned all over again.

"Baby, a nigga was slipping. I thought them bitch ass niggas shot straight from the hip, but they was lame as hell."

"Con, you fuck with these Mexicans. They moved on the north side in a big house on the corner. It's about ten of them staying in one house. They have the best dope on the block now. This might be a drug deal gone bad, baby. I'm good, just give me my part of the money or give me some product." At the moment, she'd already peeped this black Gucci bag on the side of the bed. Her instincts were telling her that everything was in that bag, and she wasn't leaving without it. Boss Chick decided not to leave and handle business with Con.

"Bitch, don't play with me. I love you with all with all my heart and soul." Con grabbed her small hands and kissed them. He told her to hold some money in her hand as he reached in the closet to get a money counting machine. She was smiling when he came out the closet and asked her for her help.

"Damn, nigga, I love your ass from the top of your head to the bottom of your feet." She kissed him on the lips.

Chapter 5

Con's eyes was on Boss Chick's fat pussy after she walked out the shower. She chuckled to herself, but she knew what she had to do to make him take a trip with her to handle some business. She smiled and licked her big lips like a freak in a local strip club, trying to suck some dick for someone. He looked directly into her pretty green eyes and grinned seductively. He grabbed her and pushed her on the bed. Her legs went wide, opening as he touched her with his hands and then put his face down there. "I'm taking this pussy tonight, baby!" He laughed.

"Oh, shit-shit-fuck! Oh, baby," she moaned, riding his face. Shit went so quickly that she ended up sitting on his face in a different position.

He pushed her off him and stuck his tongue in her pussy. He moved his tongue in and out of her pussy as she held his head like a basketball.

"I'm about to cum on your tongue, nigga. Oh, shit!" She was trying to get away from his long tongue that was deep in her pussy. "Bitch nigga, you know how to suck on some pussy. You have the best head game a bitch ever had."

He pushed all twelve and a half inches of hard dick inside her tight pussy. She came all the way unglued, loving how all the colors of the rainbow were dancing on the back of her eyelids. Her orgasm washed over her like liquid hot gold. She felt his explosion all up in her stomach. The dick was so good it had her dickmatized at the moment. Her wet pussy was going to work on his dick riding him like her life depended on it. Cash was grabbing ahold of her nice ass cheeks. He started pulling her down on him with enough force to make a bitch reconsider his dick size again.

"Now I can't stop until he makes my stomach hurt, from his big dick. Boss Chick loves pain. That's crazy as hell"

"Baby, you going to cum with me some more?" he laughed, busting another nut.

Boss Chick couldn't say anything. She squeezed her eyes shut tight, as the fog lifted, and the most beautiful paradise was laid before her. She squirted so hard that she wet the whole bed sheets up. Cash shot cum right inside her wet pussy again. She tried to remove him off of her. He pulled her against his thick chest and from her soft hands touching his strong frame, she could tell he'd been working out in somebody's gym.

"What's wrong, sweetie?"

"GiGi needs our help." He looked at her crazy in the face.

"Boss Chick, baby, a nigga will run through hell and back for you. You know damn well I'm going with you to Chi-Town. They haven't seen a nigga from North Philly get down." Cash was thinking about robbing a local bank in the process for weeks now. He needed it more money to buy a large amount of drugs to take over the hood. "Baby, will you help me rob this bank?"

She smiled. Cash was just like her, thinking the same way, but never thought he would ask her to help him. "Baby, I'm willing to do what you want a bitch to do. Cash, you have a bitch's heart and this dick belongs to me, as she grabbed a handful.

They put on some clothes then walked outside to Cash's Audi. He showed her the map on how to handle the robbery plan and how they were going to get away. He then showed her several guns they were going to use to make shit happen. He gave her a black ski mask and handed her a .357 handgun. Boss Chick was so happy that she pointed the .357 handgun in the air and fired the gun off. Cash decided that selling drugs was not enough money, so they decided that this was an excellent idea. The two individuals donned ski masks, brandished automatic weapons and pulled off. This robbery would be history in the making for them to cherish the rest of their lives.

They drove off to the local National Bank on Main Street in the center of Blytheville, Arkansas, less than twenty minutes away from where they lived. Both of them exited the vehicle and grabbed several empty duffle bags from the backseat. Once they entered the bank, the first bank teller refused to put the money in the bag by demand. Boss Chick slapped her across the head with her gun, causing the woman to fall to the floor in pain, screaming for dear life. Blood was pouring out of the side of her head. The other tellers didn't give them a problem and put the money in the duffle bag, with military precision on time, nabbing nearly three million dollars in the process as they thought by looking at the duffle bags. The exit from the bank was a thrill they would never forget. They were gone in the wind, leaving no trace of their criminal acts as they thought at the moment. As they entered the neighborhood, they decided to drop off the duffle bags at their own house to be safe in case the laws traced them with marked money. Sometimes they called each other the baddest robber in the world.

Boss Chick reached into one of the duffle bags and grabbed a couple of hundred-dollar bills off the stack to get her hair and nails done at Targie Nail Shop. In the midst of her grabbing the money while Cash was driving, they arrived at the nail shop real quick. The town was so small you could walk wherever you needed to go. As they arrived at the new shop and walked into the building, ten minutes later, the police started circling the area. All of a sudden, Boss Chick and Cash got up and walked toward their vehicle to see what was going on. Boss Chick wasn't alone in the nail shop at the time.

The officers and more police cars rushed around them and several of them were already out of their car on foot patrol. They pointed several handguns in their direction and Boss Chick started crying without a doubt and she wasn't in handcuffs yet.

"Y'all put your hands up in the air!" The police had plenty of suspects but were unable to pinpoint who was actually responsible for the robbery. They made several guesses but they were tipped in their direction and location. The obvious suspects were members of the city's growing cartel problem, and the police had good reason that this heist was committed by a gang as the efficiency and expertise suggested it. What's more, the bank had been specifically targeted, possibly by someone with inside knowledge. The police believed the suspect knew someone at the bank with inside information, but someone had tipped them off to locate the two suspects.

***

Two months later, the two suspects were caught and on trial. The witness had testified in hushed intense whispers about the cartel, so the police concluded that the cartel probably had a lookout who communicated with the thieves inside the bank. The police were relentless in their pursuit of the robbers. The suspects were released but were still under surveillance with the feds on the low. The bench trial didn't have enough evidence to hold them at the moment. Many law enforcement personnel were set up around the city and many other cities in that area. More detectives were hired to investigate the case even more, and informants with possible leads were paid to share what they knew. Public surveillance cameras were also monitored in an effort to find anything leading to the identity of the robbers. Police spent long hours reviewing footage from the cameras but were unable to finalize facial recognition, a date or anything else that could be used against the robbers. At long last, police uncovered a name that was tied to the bank robbers, Angel Smith. Throngs of officers were sent to different neighborhoods in the small town in search of Angel Smith, better known as Boss Chick, and a man named Cash. The officers didn't know his real name at the time because he wasn't a prime suspect at the moment, but he might be in the future. Cash's cousin had been working at the bank for seventeen years strong and gave Cash inside information on what to do and when to do it.

After weeks of searching, the feds finally realized that they wanted Cash too. They caught up with both of them at a local motel on the west side of town. It was a brief car chase that led to some scuffling to get them apprehended and find out Cash's real name is Russell Wells. They searched them and the vehicle, finding evidence linking them to the robbery. Both of them looked puzzled and didn't have anything to say to each other.

With Mr. Wells in custody, the feds and local law enforcement didn't have to search very hard for more members of the gang. After several hours of interrogation, RaRa was released and promised to be a star witness at the trial. When both of them were finally rounded up and arrested, the police had accomplished something miraculous in the small town. The capture of the first large scale bank robbers in the history of the city's criminal justice system.

At trial, a whole army of lawyers defended the accused. The prosecution painted a vivid picture of the crime and described how the frighteningly efficient thieves had planned and pulled off the perfect crime. As the witnesses' testimonies were heard and the lawyers debated, the jury deliberated for hours before finally coming to a verdict. In the end, all defendants were found not guilty. Cash was the ringleader and received a smile from one of the star witnesses and the jury.

The news of the trial soon spread through the small town and Memphis, TN. Many people of all walks of life were discussing the loss and crime that the court system let get away free. Many were relieved that the crime spree had been stopped, while others mourned the loss of a bank teller, due to the injury to her brain. The National Bank robbery changed the small town forever. Banks beefed up their security measures, police stations invested in maintaining better neighborhoods out of fear of a similar crime happening to them.

The First National Bank was a cautionary tale for all who heard of it. It taught people to be more aware of their surroundings and to take precautions when dealing with banks and financial institutions. It also highlighted the importance of having an extensive police force. to keep criminals in check and citizens safe.

Chapter 6

The First National Bank robbery of the city was a shockwave that continues to be felt to this day. The brazen act of violence that occurred in broad daylight highlighted the issue of crime. Putting the city on edge at the same time. In the end, society was able to take lessons away from it and move on. The suspects were caught, and no justice was done to them. This issue serves as a reminder that crime will never be fair, as well the court system. No matter how well planned or cleverly executed, criminals must face justice and pay for their crime. RaRa was not a government, as you can see. The suspects got away free and were told to leave the city for one year and not come back.

Boss Chick and Cash never mentioned anything to anyone about them leaving the town for one year. Boss Chick was supposed to leave town and check on her girlfriend and all this shit went into play. Boss Chick was ashamed to call her because they haven't had a conversation in months. Now they hit a lick, they can move anywhere and set up shop. The main thing is staying free and not harming RaRa for being a rat to the fullest to the government. They decided to move to a small town outside of Blytheville and come back and forth to sell their drugs. Most of the people around them had given up on their dreams, with many resorting to crime and others forms of immoral acts in order to make a living. Both determined to rise above the circumstances, set off on an incredible journey that would change their lives forever.

They had known each other since childhood, attended the same school and shared the same bed and dream in life. Both wanted nothing more than to provide a better life for their families and make something of themselves. One day, while sitting around at the club bar, they began to talk about ideas on what to do with the money. That's when more shit came into play. They could make a lot more money selling dope at a cheaper price than the next clique. They started off selling nickel and dime rocks when they first started before the bank robbery happened. Both of them weren't good drug dealers at the time, but since they got the money and drugs it made them go harder and harder, selling dope at a cheaper price. They had a plan that would never be forgotten, to rule the world in a small-time frame.

At first the idea sounded crazy. All they knew at the moment about methamphetamine and cocaine was this shit wasn't legal. The main thing was to get their dope already cooked up and solid, ready to sell. Most young niggas called it bricks, because they were buying them at twelve point five apiece. Maybe that was too much but they didn't care. They had access to the local drug networks in their area and knew the ins and outs of the drug trade. On top of that, if they could get in with the right connections, the money was practically guaranteed. They decided to take a risk once again. They pooled their finances to get started. They had enough money to buy several bricks and pounds of weed. Although they were amateurs, they were slowly learning the ropes and starting to make some major money, so they thought.

Despite their occasional successes, they weren't always successful. Drug dealing was a dangerous business and the risks were real. On multiple occasions they were stopped by the police and faced harsh consequences. It was during these dark hours that they called upon their inner strength and worked the same determination and drive they'd always had.

Eventually, their hard work began to pay off. When each deal they made, they were slowly but surely solidifying their place in the local drug trade. Before long, they had managed to establish themselves as legitimate dealers in the hood. Both were now making good money and were able to give back to their community. They helped to provide jobs to many people in the hood who were struggling to make ends meet. In addition, they invested some of their profits in nearby homes and setting up for financial success in the future. They were able to rise from poverty to prosperity, and their success was a beacon of hope for many in their hood. They put their lives on the line and made something of themselves. They were just fucking partners at the time because Boss Chick had a lot of friends she fucked and dealt with.

***

Toe Tag looked down at Caressa. He ran his fingers down her waist and continued up to her thick thighs. She wore nothing but a long pink 7-shirt with no panties or bra on. Her nipples were already hard and pressed against her shirt. He planted many soft kisses on her shoulder. Caressa knelt before him, giving him thunderous head. Toe Tag palmed the back of her head, grinding his dick as far as he could down her throat. "You is cold with this mouth shit," Toe Tag growled, watching as she devoured him. Her warm saliva ran down his dick, where it came to rest deep inside his boxers. He gently massaged her shoulders, feeling the nut beginning to build up. "Turn that nice ass around doggy style from the back," he instructed Caressa, wanting to feel his eleven inches sliding in and out of her wet pussy. Caressa continued to slurp and suck on Toe Tag's dick one last time. She already knew how Toe Tag liked getting his dick sucked, then gave him some pussy. The first time they had sex was when she left with him when Cross gave her a black eye that Con asked her about in the post. He bent Caressa over the couch, thumping his dick up against her ass cheeks. "You ready for this big black dick?" Toe Tag growled like a pitbull, running the tip of his dick between her ass cheeks, slowly guiding his dick into her wet pussy.

"Yes," she moaned as Toe Tag slowly pushed his dick slowly inside of her pussy. "Toe Tag," she cried out more, he continued to dive deeper, pounding harder and harder. Clap! Clap! He pounded away. "Oh baby, yessss!" she moaned then it happened for the first time in her life. She never knew what it felt like, but she knew it was something new to her body. Caressa's legs started moving uncontrollably, then it happened. She squirted so damn hard that she splashed his whole body, and the bed was wet. All she could do when he went back inside her pussy was to keep squirting. "Please stop!" But Toe Tag pounded and pounded away inside her pussy. All Caressa could say was, "Oh shit! Oh shit!" and kept moaning at the top of her lungs. Caressa enjoyed Toe Tag's dick so much that her tongue was hanging out her mouth like a dog needing water.

Toe Tag growled out loud, "I'm about to cum!" and let his cum shoot up inside her pussy like he was trying get her pregnant.

"Damn, have my sister ever fucked you like that? The next time we fuck, I'm going let you fuck me in the asshole with no grease." She laughed. Toe Tag was out for the count, asleep from the good head and pussy Caressa put on him. Caressa was throwing that ass back on him like she was riding a bull at a rodeo show in Texas.

Chapter 7

Con stood under the hot shower head, allowing the water to cascade over his body. The encounter between him and Aries added only more fuel to the fire that was already at full blaze. At times, Con didn't know if he was coming or gang. He was emotional at times, but in the next minute he was happy to be alive. The next few seconds, he'd be ready to go into kill mode with the world. After he completed his shower, he threw on some boxer shorts and retired to the front room for the night, listening to music, relaxing his mind and soul. Con thought about GiGi and he never thought about her in this way. Con's dick was getting harder second by second. Con was in coma a while ago and he dreamed of having sex with GiGi. It was good to Con as he licked his lips. Con wanted more of that good pussy. Con had a lot of time to think about his next move before he went back into his kill mode. Con listened to soft music, taking his mind far away from the bullshit in the world. It was times like this that put Con's mind at rest. Now all Con have to do was focus on getting Boss Chick back. Boss Chick was with her nigga Cash upstate or down south somewhere, who knows.

The music instantly smoothed out his mind and brought a smile to his solemn face. Con was so caught up, that he didn't hear the doorbell, it startled him out of his thoughts. Con was never the one to have company at his main crib. Only a few older family members, because Con couldn't trust the young ones out there in the streets. Con sat up on the sofa and turned the music down. He was just about to inquire about who was outside when he thought about the car that creeped past the house last night and also earlier today. Not only did whoever was behind the dark tinted window wish to keep their identity concealed, but they also wanted to make sure their presence was known. Con rushed to the table. He checked the chamber to make sure they were ready to lit off at any moment. Con made his way to the front door. "Who that be?"

"It's me, Fat Mac and Boo, just stopped by to holla at you for a minute."

Con let them come into the door and shut the behind them. "It was crazy both of them was at my crib," he said to himself. These are two wild niggas from Chi-Town. "What's good with y'all?"

"Not shit, Boo is high as hell on that good loud weed. Prey and Polo stated they will get with you tomorrow. You know how them two niggas get down. They been getting that money and fucking them white bitches across the world."

Boo looked around and saw two .45 handguns in Con's hands.

"Why you got them twins out like that, nigga?"

"It's a war out here in these streets," Con said.

"All you have to do is say the word and it's war time, but you got to get these new toys right here." Boo pulled his jacket up to show off his two FN's he had on him with 30-round clips hanging out the side of the two FN's.

"Man, you can't go wrong with this, Con." Fat Mack pulled his jacket up, showing his Uzi and extra clips. "This bitch here will make a nigga forget that he has a gun in his or her presence."

Con and Boo laughed at Fat Mack. Boo made it to the living room to sit down. Boo was so high that he was thinking out loud with his words, about killing somebody.

"Con, you have anything to drink, because Boo need to drink some kind of liquor?" Fat Mack told Boo not to smoke that love weed he got from Polo the other day in the project. You know that niggas getting that shit from them Haitian niggas in the project. That shit be gas all the time!" Fat Mack said.

Con was thinking about how he was going handle the niggas trying to murder him. One of the important things going through Con's mind was getting back to his money selling bricks on the streets.

"Thank you, you know a nigga only keep sodas around here. Go in there and see what I have. Boo, how the hell you going shoot that gun when you high as fuck right now?"

"That shit don't stop me from killing a nigga around here, player. This good weed helps me to knock a lot of niggas on their ass. A nigga's done it many times when niggas don't pay my money for my dope I gave them. You can see that I'm with the bullshit, point your finger and it's a done deal, like the mob or cartel around this bitch!"

"Shut the fuck up, player, with all that tough man shit. Keep drinking that soda, so we can go handle some business."

Fat showed a picture to Con. "This nigga owe me some money. If he don't pay me by midnight, I'm knocking him the fuck out with one hard uppercut under the chin and shooting him in the ass cheek where it hurt."

Boo had seen Fat Mack hit a nigga with a hook and knock most his teeth out at Club Tubb's. "I'm not trying go to prison behind some bullshit. Dude looked like he got in a fight with Mike Tyson."

"Do you have some goons that can branch off in Chi-Town to kill two niggas that killed Justice? Their names are Toe Tag and Aries, heavyweights."

Boo and Fat Mack looked at Con. "Man, I know them bitch ass niggas. Toe Tag be on 79th with the GD's. Some of my homies tied with his baby sister and cousin. Toe Tag think be the plug, but I really think that nigga Aries the main plug."

"Oh, he do? We will see about all that Shit. Boo, man, fuck ol' boy he can get his shit knocked off if that's what he wants."

"Nawl. Not right now!" Con said to Boo. How much do that nigga Sam owe you, Fat Mack?" Con switched the conversation real fast.

"That nigga owes me for a brick of cocaine. He owes me thirteen point five and I need that right now. Sam got money both by pussy and cars. Most of them niggas be tricking off with them bitches at the club."

"Okay, but I will pay you what he owes you at this moment. I need you to get your crew together and let them niggas know that a million dollars is over Toe Tag's head. You can contact anyone close to him."

"Damn! Con, I will kill his whole family for that price."

"Boo, I know, but you and Fat Mack going to take over shit. I'm going give y'all twenty bricks of pure cocaine and a hundred pounds of purple loud weed, Fat Mack. You know what to do with all that?"

"We about to blow up around this bitch! Boo can't smoke all the weed up with them white bitches at the strip club in Memphis on Brooks Street."

"You right, my dude."

"Con, I have the goons for that job."

"You talking about them young niggas in Arkansas on the east side of town that killed a hundred and fifty people in less than one hour. That's mob shit. Most of them nigga in the feds from the 2015 Blind Justice Operation in Blytheville, Arkansas. My nigga Tubb in Yazoo Federal Prison now for selling drugs and will be coming home in a couple of years. That nigga was the man, and he had written several books while in there like *Consequence of the Game*, *Plug's Ruthless Daughter*, social justice empowerment and children's book called *Bounce Bunny and Friends*. That nigga's signed with a cat named Cash that's been in the book game for decades."

"Yep. Them niggas don't play at all. They even had the police, probation officer and county workers on payroll. I believe they went to the feds also."

"I know that, but they got a cartel group of killers that will die for him." Boo was puzzled about Aries' members at the moment.

"If they ride with him, they will die with him, point blank."

"I like how you talking, my nigga!"

"You're right about that. Loyalty over else around this bitch. You can take that to the bank on everything, for life," Con said with a smile. "Fat Mack, you mentioned that Polo be kicking it with them Haitian boys, right?"

"Yep. We going to see how things play out. Polo got shit locked in his hood. The city is gone on that fentanyl mix. That shit will get you a lot of fed time, especially if someone dies from it. When niggas started selling that shit? What happened to the rocks, weed and cocaine niggas was selling in the hood? Niggas selling meth now, trying to dodge the feds, and now the feds giving a lot of time for meth because blacks are selling it."

"Holla at me tomorrow morning," Con said, "your shipment will be here!"

"Okay, will do, bruh." Fat Mack and Boo left Con's crib real fast without giving him a handshake or hug. "Man, we about to take the game over, Boo."

"Show you right, Fat Mack. Bro, I need you to take me over this bitch crib. She be taking dick everywhere, including in her asshole with no grease. The head game will make your toes curl up." He laughed to himself about the whole situation.

Chapter 8

GiGi had just touched down in Chi-Town looking for Con, but when she got there, people at the hospital stated he'd checked himself out. "Oh, I know where he could be. Whenever it came time to put in work or set a nigga up to get killed, he was down to handle his part. He feels like I owe him my whole life. We met under similar circumstances. Con was in Memphis seven years ago, pulling on some drug dealer when he ran into one of my trap spots out there. The nigga Con was there to rob, had me between his legs, jacking his big dick off. Come to find out Con was my cousin, and I was younger than him. At the end of this, Con killed that nigga. I was twenty-five at the time. I ended up coming back to Chicago with him. Since then, we've formed a brother and sister thang bond that's unbreakable, but we only had things going that will blow your mind thinking about the past."

"You okay, shorty?" the bartender asked, snapping GiGi out of her reverie.

"Yeah, I'm good."

"Why you over here by yourself?"

"Anyways," she said, after looking him up and down.

"Damn, it's like that?"

She yelled, "You can't do nothing with a bitch like me. I mean, look at you and look at me. Really, you in here looking like Farmer John with a plain Jane ass outfit you got at the corner store. Nigga, please!"

"Ha-ha, nah, you good. I ain't tripping," Tyson said, rocking a smile.

"Nah, nigga, you is tripping, been tripping since you came here looking like a clown," she laughed.

He was mad. "Do you know the fuck I am around here, bitch?"

Before Tyson could say another word, GiGi hit him with a swift two-piece that put him on his ass. "Now, nigga, who's the bitch now? You got knocked on your ass like a bitch."

His friends just looked at her and then went and picked their friend off the ground and exited the club. She was mad that Con wasn't there to help her, but she hit their mans with that two-piece on point. What she didn't know was that Con was off in the same club with her, but by the time he got over there, he saw three muscular dudes walking out the club, talking shit to each other. Con saw GiGi and he knew that she could deal with ole boy. Con came up behind her and wrapped his strong arms around her waist real tight.

"Get the fuck off me, nigga!" She spun around and saw it was Con. She rolled her eyes about five times and turned around, playing hard to get and that's the way she liked it. She walked with Con to his car and got in. "Con, don't try play me like a bitch and take me home." Con sat there looking at her a few minutes before pulling off. They didn't say anything to each other on the ride to his house.

"What are you going to do about that bitch, Karen?" she screamed.

"Hold up, you are not going to handle me like this."

GiGi narrowed her eyes at Con.

"Girl… don't think about it. I will bust you in the lips real fast, bitch." Before he could say more, she tackled him to the floor and somehow got his arms pinned under her knees, which put her pussy in his face.

"Nigga, I should pound your ass out right now." She slapped him several times. "Apologize, nigga, and kiss this pussy cat." She moved up until her pussy was in his mouth.

He stuck his tongue out and flicked it across her clit. "Ow, nigga! Oh my God," was all she could get out of her mouth before Con tossed her on the floor.

"You want to play?" Con lifted her red dress over her head and nudged his knee between her thick legs, forcing them open.

"I swear to God, you better not let me up. I'm going to fuck you up!"

"Oh, you like that rough sex shit? Your little pussy wet right now." Con climbed between GiGi's legs. He rubbed his hand and his hard dick head up and down her slit. She moaned loud as fuck. They looked in each other's eyes, as he placed his dick at her wet opening. Con was about to enter her when somebody knocked at the front door, bring them to their senses. "Who is that?" Con said, while GiGi was getting herself together. She forgot to put her panties back on, so she ran to the bathroom and hid them in the trash can and came back out.

"It's me, Prey and Polo. Well, you said holla at you in the morning. Well, my nigga, it's 7:00 AM as you can see. What better way to come by before the birds get up and eat?"

When GiGi peeked outside the front door, Prey's eyes were all over her nice round ass.

"Where the fuck you get that beautiful woman at?"

"Chill out, man."

"Damn, GiGi."

She looked at Prey and said, "Nigga, you my brother, don't play with me like that. Keep your eyes to yourself. I don't know your friend, so it's best he do the same." She rolled her eyes at Polo and Prey. She started looking at Con.

"GiGi, take your ass in the bedroom and leave these niggas alone please."

"Damn you, nigga." She walked toward the bedroom with her ass jiggling in that dress with no panties on, showing what her mother gave her.

"I know what, y'all niggas. We going to get that shipment to your real soon." Con was mad as fuck at GiGi. She just sat in the corner looking mad and refused to go into the bedroom. Con wished he could've gotten that pussy before they came over to the crib.

"Con, what it do, my dude?"

"I'm good right now."

"What's popping around here?" Polo asked.

"Wishing I had your hands, so I can cut mine off."

"You got Chris Rock jokes right now, nigga?"

"Oh, you know I know you got your city on lock out here."

Con smiled at this. "Man, I want more than just one state on lock. I won't be happy until I get more surrounding cities. "Okay, I'm pretty sure you two know why you here. I need to be sold on why I should deal with you!"

Prey was the first one to speak up. "My city runs through. me. I supply the majority of my city, but with you in my corner, I'd be able to solidify my spot in my state. At the same time, you'd gain another state and a crew full of hungry wolves and go-getters."

Con had to really give Prey a smile when he was done, because he talked like a real drug boss. "Polo, what you have to say, my nigga?"

"Well, you know my resume speaks for itself. I took my state from the lowest point and from the last three niggas that was holding it down. I did it by myself. I earned my name and strips... Plus, my hustle game is like nothing the world's seen before. I was the first young nigga in my hood and crew with a 2023 Bentley Continental, V8. I dare anyone in my hood to say that I'm lying."

"Now we have that all out the way. From this day forth, your beef is mines and vice versa. Whatever you need as far as work, holla at GiGi. She have great prices on everything you might need."

"Oh, hell yeah, nigga."

THE PLUG'S RUTHLESS DAUGHTER 3 | TONY DANIELS

"But she is a girl," Polo said out loud.

"My dude, she is a main weapon on this team."

GiGi looked at Polo with fire in her eyes.

"I'm that bitch. You know, nigga, my pussy get wet for putting niggas on their back. GiGi will kill a nigga in a heartbeat because that will also make her cum back-to-back." GiGi got up and exited the room for good this time.

"Con, I would love to have a goon on my team like her."

Con laughed. "Polo, it takes loyalty and a lot of hard work to have somebody like her around that will body a nigga in a second."

Polo just nodded his head, because he understood the street code that Con was giving to him. "I feel you on that, Con, and I thank you for the advice, big homie. Prey, when do we get to this bag? Why GiGi be on killer mode so damn much. She be on one when it comes Con, and that's great."

"GiGi just got upset that I almost died from fuckin' with a no-good bitch that don't mean shit to me or her. She hadn't heard from her friend Boss Chick, who is making big boss moves. GiGi said I would be safe with her, and she is like a little sister to me." All the time, Con's been trying to fuck her brains out on the low.

"Well… okay, but I think it's more to the story than you telling us, Con. We will holla at your ass later, nigga."

"Okay. You and Polo going to meet us at the safe house at 9:00 pm? Fat Mack and Boo will be there too. This is a fresh start of a great team about to blow up more."

Polo looked at Prey and told him to drop him off at his car so he could handle some business.

Con called GiGi to come out the bedroom. She came and stood in front of him. "Come a little closer, baby!" He grabbed her soft body and sat her on the couch on a nice Gucci pillow. She jumped into his lap, facing him.

"We almost fucked up bad." It didn't help that her dress hem came up and she was showing nothing but pussy. GiGi's pussy was shaved bald head, with a big clit to match. She never went back into the bathroom to get the underwear she threw in the trash can and covered up. The scent of her Chanel perfume went up Con's nostrils and made him feel like fucking her even more, if she would give him a chance. Con felt her adjust until she was sitting on the length of his dick, which started throbbing and jumping up against her pussy. She cocked her back and humped forward ever so slightly. Con didn't press his fingers together. He didn't know if it was intentional. or accidental. GiGi pressed her forehead against his.

"Do you love me?"

"Yeah, baby, I do for real. I love you and you will always be my heart and soul!"

She leaned down until her lips brushed against his lips. "I am your little sister and you trying to put all this dick inside me," she said as she grabbed his dick with her hands.

Con began to shake. "When it comes to you, some rules go out the back door." He smiled.

GiGi pressed her juicy lips against his and dropped all her weight into his lap. She felt the length and thickness of him throbbing against her ass cheeks, and pussy. Her thick thighs spread just a little bit. "."She licked his lips and turned all the way around until her back was against his chest. She rocked back and forth, giving him a subtle lap dance.

Con moaned and sucked on the back of her neck. He took his hands and slid them inside her pussy. He realized that her pussy couldn't take his big finger, so he inserted two little fingers. Con lifted her up and lowered her back down, slowly sliding his large dick inside her tight little pussy.

GiGi moaned. "Baby, we cannot do this, it's not right." She lifted and squeezed his big dick. She stroked his dick and looked at how fat and found it was. Her mouth was wide open when she saw how long and fat his dick was, and about to go inside her pussy. "I cannot let you put all that meat inside me, big boy. I will suck it for you, if that's cool with you."

Con just looked at her. "Do whatever you want to do to me."

She pulled up closer to Con and put her pussy lips on his dick even more. She groaned at the feeling of Con's skin. Her twerking persisted.

Con's dick sawed in and out of her pussy without penetrating her too much. In a matter of minutes, Con's entire lap was soaking wet with her wetness. Con was shaking so bad, before he knew what he was doing, Con had her bent over the chair with her face in a crazy direction. Con's face was inside of her crack hole, licking up and down her crease hungrily. Con kept eating until she screamed and came all over his face. He then turned her around again and his knees were against her chest. He ate her pussy while she shook and shook, cumming back-to-back, screaming about how much she loved him.

Con's chin was dripping with cum juice. He squeezed his dick, stroking it, yearning to put it inside of her, cumming the fourth time.

She stood on shaky legs with his cum running down her thick legs. She rubbed her bald head pussy with her small hands. Both of GiGi's nipples were standing up on her chest like rocks. Hard dick was about to go inside her pussy. "Con, we can't go further with this."

Con nodded from his position. He pulled her back to him and kissed her gap again. His tongue eased inside of her lips. She placed her foot on the couch and took ahold of his head humping with her eyes closed.

"Nigga, I'm supposed to be your little sister."

"Aww. Fuck… shit, you not."

GiGi screamed, as she pushed Con away and fell to the carpet convulsing as a massive orgasm rocked her body. "Aww shit, this feels good. Damn, this feels good!"

Con stood over her, dick swinging from side to side. He wiped his mouth. "Damn, a nigga gotta go take a real cool shower right now, because if I don't, we will end up fucking again." He hurried away to do what he said he had to handle, gathering his clothes together for the shower.

She made her way to her feet. Her chest was beating heavily. "Yeah, Con, I'll get into the shower after you're done." She placed her arms back into the loopholes of her dress, putting it on. GiGi forgot about her panties that were still in the bathroom trash can. A trail of cum rolled down her legs, all the way to her ankles. She wiped the cum with one of Con's new Polo shirts that he got for his birthday. The rest of the cum she wiped with her fingers and stuck it into her mouth. "Damn, there's something wrong. I'm not your average freak." She licked her tongue out.

A loud knock on the front door scared her half to death. She took a moment to gather herself, then her cellar phone was ringing in her purse. She grabbed her purse and saw it was Boss Chick. She answered the phone. "Hello?"

"GiGi, I know you hear a bitch knocking at the front door. I know your ass in there trying to get Con to fuck and suck on you." She opened the front door without saying one word. GiGi smiled, because she knew what she was up to.

Boss Chick looked at GiGi. "Damn, bitch! Con had your ass in here fucking up the house and it smell like sex in here. Spray something, bitch!"

GiGi looked at Boss Chick and Cash. "You two need to go get a motel room, not here. Bitch, I will at holla at you when I get out the shower." She still remembered Con was in there already but she was trying to shake Boss Chick and her nigga to leave. "For the record on the street, no we didn't, but Con ate my pussy real good and right now you have a nigga with you."

Boss Chick looked at Cash. "Baby, you ready to go? This bitch's mind is in a dark place right now. She can't take no dick, because her cherry never been popped." She laughed at GiGi.

"Bitch, if you'd seen this nigga's little dick, or should I say large dick, you wouldn't be saying shit right now. I had to use two hands to hold it and wish you could of been there to help me out." Cash didn't want to hear about another nigga's dick and he was ready to leave the house after their comments."

"GiGi, baby girl, I am good on dick right now. My man got a lot of pipe to lay when we get back to the motel room!" Cash smiled at his woman, knowing she was talking good about him in front her so-called friend.

"Okay… bye, bitch. I will be there in four hours or less, so be ready," GiGi said.

"That will give me enough time to get some dick and a little rest after we get done fucking. Bitch, you know I like to ride his dick backwards with no hands, like a Boss Bitch." She walked out the front door holding her man's hand like they were in love for many years.

GiGi stood there waiting until Boss Chick's Audi was gone down the road out of sight. GiGi pulled her dress over her head and rubbed her pussy and licked her long tongue out again. She was ready to go another round, her pussy was still wet. She took the stairs one at a time and opened the bathroom door where Con was taking a shower.

Con stood there with his eyes closed, pumping his piece back and forth in his hands, thinking about GiGi. He groaned ever so slightly. He squeezed his eyelids tighter and tighter. When the shower curtain got pulled back, he froze like a deer in headlights. He thought that GiGi was in the front room waiting on him to get out the shower, but he was wrong about that.

She stepped into the shower with Con and adjusted the temperature on the water. "Con, I'm right here with you," she said as he jumped from the hot water hitting his body. "You don't have to do that any more with your hands." She took off her dress and turned around with her back to him. His rock-hard long dick went right between her ass cheeks, forcing it further into her asshole, causing her to jump and make a loud sound you never heard before, like in a movie.

"What are you doing, GiGi?" he asked as she moved around and rubbed her booty all over his hard dick that started to elongate the more it touched her beautiful skin. He was in love with GiGi and Boss Chick on the cool.

"We are not doing nothing wrong at this point, baby." This was Con's first time realizing just how thick she was.

"GiGi, you're driving me crazy right now. You gotta get your ass out of here before you cross the line even more."

"No, we ain't, Con. Trust a bitch, I got this."

When GiGi pulled off the dress she had on, she revealed her bare headed pussy that Con loved the most. The water from the shower rained down on them, causing it to glisten. She spread her pussy lips with two of her fingers, exposing her pink pussy to him. "Look, juicy pussy, nigga. I know you want some more of this pussy." She took his dick and rubbed it up and down between her pussy lips. The feeling of Con's flesh against hers made her weak in the knees "Aww, shit… this is it right here, nigga!" She slapped Con across the head as she felt her knees shake even more. Con told her to bend over as she bounced her ass back and forth on his dick. She suckled on her bottom lips and shivered. Con pushed his hips forward and slid in four inches of dick inside her. Her heat scared him. She was so tight and her pussy was hot, the main thing was that she was dripping so much on his dick that he started to moan and moan, sounding like a dog to her out the gate.

"GiGi, baby, what are you doing to me?" She moaned as he slid a few more inches inside. Her She leaned forward and pulled his dick out of her pussy.

"We have to stop here," Con said, trying to make her keep going.

They decided to come to an agreement and get out of the shower. She walked out the bathroom with her thick ass jiggling and her titties bouncing on her thick, yet slim frame. When she stepped in the bedroom to get a new pair of panties out of her book bag, by the time she was done, Con was right behind her in the bedroom like a dog in heat. She turned around and saw him. "Con, are you mad at me?"

Con held her by her small hands and grabbed her ass cheek with his left hand. He kissed her soft lips. Why would I be, fine ass?"

"I'm sure it seemed like I'm teasing you, but that's not my intention at all. I wanna be there with you, every part of me does, as you can see. I know it's wrong, no matter how I really want you, my homie loved you with all her heart. She also stated that she will be at the motel room for several hours with her dude and will be leaving going back home to handle some business. She really don't know that we been fucking, so keep this shit on the low."

"Well, I'm not mad at you. What type of real man would be upset with you? Boss Chick and I have some work to do and to be honest, we been messing around for a minute and she stated that she going to leave Cash and come back home. That's the reason she really came to my crib. That nigga just in the way as you can see, baby." He kissed her lips again and rubbed all over her booty and squeezed. It was like a soft pillow on a bed. "I love you too much to ever be mad at you, queen."

She leaned down and placed her forehead to his. "How much do you want me?"

Con locked eyes with her. She knew she was driving Con insane. "Really don't know the answer to that right now, but my feelings are deep for you!"

"Just be honest when it comes to us. How much?" She was humping into him slowly, but firmly.

"A damn lot, little sister, or should I call you babe?" Con slid his middle finger inside her pussy, making her make a loud moaning, sound through the air.

"Ah shit! Ah shit! You know when we were in the shower together, baby?"

"Yes?"

"You popped my cherry. That's why I leaned and pulled you out. You had around eight inches of hard steel dick in a bitch's stomach at the time. You had a lot of inches left to give me. I can't take all that dick. I wonder how Boss Chick handle all that dick," she said as she grabbed his manhood. Con's dick began to jump.

"T-that's to you," he stuttered, imagining the feeling of her. He also was thinking about Boss Chick coming back to the crib later on.

She scooted upward and took ahold of his dick and eased the head of it past her pussy lips with her mouth wide open. She moved down until she locked her body up. "Ugh, shit!"

Con grabbed a handful of her ass. "Damn, baby, your pussy wet as hell." He stuck his finger inside her. Doing this took his dick to a whole new level.

"I know, Con." She slid down about nine inches out of thirteen inches of his dick in her mouth, moving up and down with her mouth open. Her saliva ran down the side of her mouth. "I'm so sorry, baby. Oh shit! Un! Un! Un! Right there, baby! Con!" was all she could say, that's all that came out of her mouth. When she went back up, she stated to Con, "Nigga, I'm about to take all this dick." She popped back down in his lap and swallowed all thirteen inches like a porn star, then she straddled him, bouncing up and down repeatedly, taking all of his dick at one time. "I love this big dick, Con." She started to make loud sounds, as she looked down at his dick from the pain she was dealing with. "Uh-uh, big brother, you in a bitch's stomach for real, right now." She shuddered as she took the beating. Her tongue was hanging out of her mouth. He slammed back into her pussy, but she slammed back into him as she struggled to catch her breath. "Mmmm! Uh-uh, shit! Oh, Con, Oh Con, you're too deep in my stomach. I'm not a thot anymore. My pussy is not that deep. Can't you tell by the way it feels?"

"You are not leaving me?" Every time he pounded more in her stomach, she groaned louder.

"A bitch not going anywhere. I love you! Fuck me, Con, fuck your pussy, baby. Unn, shit, I'm cumminng!" She was in tears after busting several nuts. She felt Con dining in her little pussy. "You can have me and Boss Chick. I will play my role and not say anything!"

Con tightened his grip up on her and started fucking her so hard that the headboard began to slam to the wall with a steady tapping sound. There was a huge puddle of secretions under their sweaty bodies. He stroked her faster and faster while she moaned at the top of her lungs. She scratched his lower back, screaming for help. Con plunged deeper and deeper before he growled and pulled out of her, pumping his dick. His semen flew all over her stomach and pussy. She hopped on all fours and took ahold of his dick, sucking it in her mouth. She started licking it like a sucker as she moaned. He dumped all his seeds in her mouth. She fell on her back breathing hard. Con laid beside her and pulled over to him, kissing her fat lips. "You good? You sure you ain't gon' feel some type of way about me when we around other people?"

She shook her head. "Naw, Con, or at least I hope not, player. You know Boss Chick and Cash come over while you were in the shower. We had a long conversation, but I mentioned to them, you would call her in four hours or less." She laughed.

"Oh, you did?"

"Why do we need them?"

"They with us. Boss Chick is the devil. Her man is the devil also. I heard about all the shit they have done and right now they're buying a lot of bricks of cocaine. They got their part of the city in control." GiGi decided that she would get her belongings and leave to let them handle business.

***

While at the motel room, Boss Chick and Cash decided that she would stay there to handle business with Con and he would head out home. Cash really didn't like being around Con, and though that Con was fuckin around with his girl. They lay there for the night and Cash waited for the morning to hit. But he was impatient, so he decided to get on the highway and leave.

"Baby, I love you, and you be careful on the highway and I will see you soon." They kissed each other and Cash walked out the door. She grabbed the phone and call Con. "Hello."

"What's up, baby?" Con answered in a soft tone.

"Not much. Cash just left the room and went back home. So, I'm on my way to your crib. Is that bitch GiGi still over there?"

"Nawl, she gone and she is like a little sister to me. I will never let anyone hurt her, babe. I got the shipment in, so come over and let's handle this business."

"Okay."

Chapter 9

Thirty minutes later, Boss Chick arrived at Con's crib. She rang the doorbell three times before he let her in with a fat wet kiss on her lips. Boss Chick was so excited she dropped her belongings at the door and started during the Money Dance at the front door. Con picked up her bags and carried them to the kitchen. She followed behind him with a big smile like she won the lottery. Con reached in the kitchen closet and grabbed a duffle and many other tools and handed them to Boss Chick. He watched over Boss Chick as they weighed the cocaine the Mexican connection had sent.

"Everything's in order," Con said as she pulled the two Fendi suitcases on the cart and wheeled them over to the table. Con sat with the two beautiful couriers that Frank had sent. Boss Chick was surprised because Con told her that nobody was there but him.

"You'll find a million dollars in each of those," Con said, turning to face Shelia, who raised her hand in a mock salute. "Take a look inside."

Though she knew it wasn't necessary, Shelia quickly scanned through the contents of each suitcase, then polished the rest of her drink off and stood. She gave Con an appeasing look, winked and tossed a phone number on the kitchen table. "The next time you're in town, make sure to put my number to use." She cast him a flirtatious glance, and to guarantee that he would give her a call, she put an extra twist in her hips as she sashayed out of the kitchen.

Reading the digits with little to no interest, Con balled the piece of paper up and tossed it into the ashtray. Con was used to gorgeous women throwing themselves at him, so Shelia's number didn't mean shit to him, period.

Immediately placing his mind back on the kilos stacked around him, Con grabbed his cell phone and dialed Fat Mack's number. Shelia and any other bitch have to wait. Money was the only thing he had on his heart at the moment, and he knew that Fat Mack would want at least twenty kilos of cocaine. Most of this will be on consignment like Con promised them. Con heard a beep on his line. Con clicked over and snapped into the receiver, receiving a "What the fuck!" He listened to the urgent ramblings of one of his workers on the other end of the phone and immediately flew into a rage. "What the hell do you mean they killed everyone but Thug?" Cutting the person's reply short, Con screamed, "Fuck him and his motherfucking tongue! If he allowed some niggas to just walk up in establishment and take me for a million dollars, sixty keys of cocaine and thirty bricks of heroin, he should have made them kill him along with the rest of them bitches! Better yet, kill him! And I want some answers about this shit immediately."

Click!

**

"Nigga, your ass is too cold!" They roared in laughter, referring to the tongue that sat on the glass table in front of them. Joining in the laughter with others, he said, the nigga was popping too much shit for me not to take it. Now, I believe he'll shut the fuck up!"

"Yeah, I imagine he will." Karen snickered, placing the money and drugs they had taken into their respective bags. Lowering his voice a decibel or so, he spoke in a low tone. "Karen, I split everything between us. You have over a half-million in cash in the bag. The keys of cocaine and heroin

will be shipped wherever you need my crew to carry them."
They had hidden some money and only showed Karen a little
bit of it.

Thug stared at Karen appreciatively and smiled at the
thought that even though she was on his team, Con had no
understanding of what he was really after. Drugs and the
game no longer meant anything to Thug. He had enough
money put away to be comfortable for a long period of time.
"I'm rich, bitch."

"What the fuck you happy about?" She pushed the bag
filled with drugs back to Thug. "You keep that shit nigga and
split it up amongst your small crew members.

"I'm good, my nigga!" Seeing the questioning look in her
eyes, Thug boasted, "I'm rich little sister!"

***

Con pulled up to the spot. He exited his vehicle and
immediately pointed in the direction of a large, tri-level blue
house that belonged to him. Although they weren't expecting
his arrival, Con still scanned the layout of the house in order
to put together the perfect plan that would accomplish his
goals. He removed his Gucci coat and jewelry and laid them
in the front seat of his car. Con placed a black 9mm in his
hand with an extra clip and jacked a round into the chamber.
He opened the car door, allowing the cold air to rush into the
warm car. Sprinting in a low gear, crouching manner across
the frozen grass, he made it to the backyard of the house
without alerting barks from the neighborhood dogs. Con's
adrenaline was pumping hard as hell.

Con was here to make them pay the piper. Nothing would
stop Con from accomplishing his task. He moved slowly and
the crashing sound that followed was loud and thunderous as
the back door exploded inward. Moving with lightning
speed, he entered the house and ran towards the candlelit
bedroom.

Thug and Karen were immersed in the heated sudsy water of the whirlpool, as soft music soothed them with her beautiful rendition of love music. The numerous candles that lit the bedroom gave it a romantic setting, but it was the feeling of her body gliding slowly and down on his own that made him forget his earlier worries. The euphoric feeling of her center and the sweet kisses she rained all over his face and neck between moans and pleasurable whimpers, gave him an invincible feeling.

Karen tossed her head back as she rode Thug's dick in the way that she knew he would love. Karen slammed herself down on him hard and fast. The loud clapping sound that their flesh made when they collided was a turn on to her and more. Biting down on her lip, she closed her eyes tightly at the feeling of approaching orgasm!

Boom! Boom! Boom!

The sound resonated throughout the house, halting their movements. Their eyes were suddenly wide open. The fear of the unknown could be seen within them. Pushing Karen off of him and into the sudsy water, they jumped out of the whirlpool. Running, he slipped and fell headfirst on the red marble tile with a loud thump. Nervously scurrying back to his feet, he continued his mad dash to the bedroom. He realized that if he planned to make it through the night, he would have to reach the .45 Smith & Wesson handgun that lay on the dresser.

The heavy footfalls Thug heard nearing the closed door indicated that more than one person was headed in his direction. His time was limited if he didn't reach his weapon soon. Moving with the speed of a leopard, he dove across the bed at the exact moment the bedroom door flew open with an ear shattering force. Only inches away from the chrome automatic, he heard the unmistakable voice that had haunted many of his dreams through the years.

"Touch it, and I'll empty this whole clip in your ass, bitch nigga!" Con hissed in a cold deadly tone that left no doubts as to his intentions, with his fingers lingering only inches from the Glock turned in the direction of his old friend.

At the sight of Con standing in the doorway with a 9mm trained on him, the only thought that came to mind was, *it had to come down to this sooner or later.* Figuring that he was about to die anyway, he decided that if he had to go, he might as well try. *I'm going to die and take someone along for the ride.* Suddenly smiling at the circumstance that he now found himself in, they began to chuckle. Maintaining eye contact, his eyes narrowed, giving him a sinister appearance. Without warning or regret, he reached for the weapon.

Bullet after bullet tore through Thug's upper torso, spraying blood and chunks of his flesh all over the sheets and wall as they exited. As promised, Con emptied the whole clip into his body. The loud sound of the 9mm and Karen's shrill screams filled the room.

Naked and shivering, Karen cowered in the corner of the bathroom. Tears streamed down her face as she grieved for this, the death she knew awaited her once the longer breathed. Hearing bootsteps approaching, Karen looked at the face that now represented nothing more than demise. Con was the devil, and the evil look on his face said it all. Her time had arrived.

Con allowed his gaze to momentarily linger on Karen's luscious frame. He felt an old sexual urge that he thought had caused to exist long ago. Her sweet, brown frame hadn't lost a single drop of the allure he had once found so tempting. After all the years that he had been away, she still presented a picture of utter perfection. Shit, to be honest, he'd just fucked her before Boss Chick had a wreck. Second-guessing his original plan, he felt that if he were to put a bullet into such perfection, he wouldn't be able to live with himself.

Karen hugged herself tightly, as it bracing herself for the inevitable bullets. She opened her eyes and a look of surprise crossed her face, when the burning look in Con's eyes was the only thing that bore into her body. Drawing strength from his apparent appraisal, she began to speak in a pleading, trembling voice in hopes of saving her life. "Babe, p-please... don't hurt me! I-I know...I know... I know I fucked up many times before, but you were always on a bitch's mind, no matter what."

Con lowered his gun a little bit, and this seemed to boost her confidence. She began to speak even faster to live. "Con, we've been through too much together. I know you haven't forgotten how good we once were together," she stated desperately. "I still love you, nigga. Con, I mean it, and not even you can execute the woman who loves you!"

"You're right," Con sighed, dropping the arm that held the Glock to his side. "Karen, I can't kill you, baby."

By the sudden gleam he noticed in her eyes, he could tell that once again, she felt as though she had got her way again. Regardless of who Katen crossed and hurt in the process, she never expected to receive any punishment for her action. *The bitch tried to kill me with black mamba poison.* Shaking his head in disgust, he could no longer understand what he had seen in her in the first place.

Turning to walk out of the bathroom, Con said the words that he knew would wipe the gleam out of her eyes and make her heart skip several beats. "Karen, I may not be able to kill you, but my girlfriend Boss Chick will!" Boss Chick surprisingly came out from nowhere, wrapped up in a bandage around her hand, arms, and legs. Con walked right past her. "Kill that low down bitch, baby!"

The last words Con heard from Karen were, "No! Please don't do this to me now! Please! I'll do anything, Con!" As Con entered the hallway, her pleas were silenced by the loud weapon that erupted. Picking up his pace, he recalled the words he had said to Karen on a sandy beach in the past. Con asked Karen never to cross him. Now, it was evident that she hadn't taken him seriously. Look what happened.

Con and Boss Chick went to one of Con's trap spots to grab a few essentials that they would need. Con's trap house was right off Maple in West Rose Apartments. Con was always in close proximity to his crew. He grabbed several duffle hugs from a small closet and tossed it to her.

"Thanks, babe, but I'd rather have a long blade." She looked at the empty bag. She saw an Army stamp on the side of the duffle bag. She wondered if Con had spent time in the military before coming into the drug game.

Con removed the book, and there was a clicking sound, followed by the bookshelf folding inward to reveal the hidden room behind. The room was barely the size of the closet, but it was what it held that made Boss Chick's eyes go wide. There were at least two dozen weapons, pistols, rifles, swords and axes. Con had a small armory hiding in his apartment.

"This strikes me as the sexist person who was preparing for war that he claims he didn't believe coming," Boss Chick said, inspecting the weapons.

"A nigga been preparing for war since the day he was brought into this world. I never said I didn't believe it was coming, just didn't expect it to come here," Con replied. Con started pulling weapons from their racks and putting them into the duffle bags, mostly blades and a few handguns. Con also added what looked like a pipe bomb that was heavily bubble wrapped.

Boss Chick selected two big pistols, a Glock and a P89. Part of her was tempted to snatch the AR-15 that Con had on the wall too. It would serve them well if they found themselves outnumbered while trying to escape, but it would also slow them down. In light of the situation, she felt like they would have to make their exits as speedy as possible. With the guns tucked into the holsters at her hips, Boss Chick was ready. She was about to leave the weapon closet when something caught her eye. It was a sharp sword with a blade that thickened as it went and curved to a thin needle. She took it from the hook on the wall and held it in her small hands. She let her eyes roam over the finely crafted weapon. They would be helpful, but that was more her speed. Its design reminded her of a stingray, and that's what she decided to name it. Now armed, the two headed out the door.

"What's your plan?" she asked once they had left the apartment.

"Once we're away from here, to get to the safe house as fast as we can and hope we can catch Aries' ass before he walks into whatever trap's been laid for him. He was headed for Atlanta. It we there before nightfall, baby."

"Sounds good to me, but there's only one problem. You promise me you will fuck the shit out of me and suck on this pussy when this shit over with?" She grabbed a handful of her pussy with a smile.

"Damn, that pussy fat. You know I'm going to handle all that and some more. We aren't going through the gates. We'll use the same way that got you into here last time to get out. The next town is only a few miles over. Once we reach it, we can procure transportation to Atlanta."

And if the tunnels are guarded as well?" Boss Chick asked a stupid question.

"Then we fight like hell." He patted the duffle bags. They continued from there to freedom, which took them past Aries' quarters. The two guards who normally stood vigil outside his door were gone, which struck her as odd. As Boss Chick thought on it, she hadn't seen much of anyone since their war with the first cartels. The place had been buzzing with activity earlier, but now it felt deserted.

"We come back later and catch Aries another way, baby. Let's get back to the apartment."

"Okay," she replied quickly with a big smile on her beautiful face.

Chapter 10

Two Hours Later

"Hmmm," Con moaned as the feeling of warmth tightened around his strength. He could feel the veins popping out of his dick, as his dick grew inside of her wet mouth. Being awakened out of his sleep to the best head game of his life was like heaven and some more shit. Boss Chick was good for not knocking before she entered the bedroom. Con had meant to pull her to the side and discuss what had happened, to prevent it from going further.

In a conscious state, he would have been able to decline this favor, but she had caught him off guard. Boss Chick had slipped into his king size bed while he was asleep and wrapped her sexy lips around his large dick. As Con brought his hands to her head, he fisted her hair as he straightened his long legs, while curling his toes in ecstasy,

"Shit," he whispered. Con had so much tension built up in him that he could feel himself pulsating in her mouth. Her tongue circled his dick head, causing every nerve ending in his body to awaken. Her hands reached up and rubbed over his chest, while her head traveled south, and her tongue massaged his dick. Con sucked in a sharp breath when he felt her tongue dip too far and he tightened his grasp on her hair to pull her up. He finally opened his eyes and lifted his head to the most beautiful sight he had ever seen.

"Baby," she said with a pretty smile.

"Boss Chick?" he softly whispered. Con wanted to think he was dreaming by calling her name softly... that she was a figment of Con's erotic imagination but the pleasure he felt was too real... too familiar to be fake. "What are you—"

"Shhh," Boss Chick whispered, as she placed a finger over his lips and pushed him back onto the expensive bed sheets. She pulled her Chanel dress over her head and spun her body around so that she could mount Con backwards. She snaked her hips, and he followed as her waist and behind wound to a silent beat. By the time her depth drowned Con, he could barely hold off the orgasm. A rush washed over them both as her mouth fell open in an O shape and she drew in a sharp breath as Con stretched her walls. Con was thick and strong. The feelings of his hands on her hips set the tone as she began to rock and roll slowly. Con had a front row seat, and he had to bite into his bottom lip to keep himself from losing his cool and moaning too fucking loud. She rode him like she was a star cowgirl in a movie. Each time she bucked backward, he saw the pink inside of her pussy bloom as her voluptuous ass cheeks spread. This nigga had some good eyes. It was a beautiful sight to behold. Con reached out and palmed her backside, massaging it as she made his length disappear and reappear, again and again in her slippery abyss. Boss Chick was warm and the honey scent invaded Con's senses was the sweetness that only a woman could possess.

"Let's play a game," she whispered, as she turned her neck and looked back at Con. The pretty girl look in her beautiful eyes was seductive yet flirtatious, and she subtly looked down at her own ass she twisted her hips simultaneously. She smirked because she knew that Con loved every moment of her sex play.

Con hadn't been inside Boss Chick's pussy in a minute liked he used to, because she been upset with him. He held his nut for a minute. Boss Chick tightened her walls until her muscles shook, begging for release, but she kept them locked around his dick. "Have you been giving my dick away again, Con?" she asked.

"You know this your big dick, baby," Con replied as he sucked his teeth, toes curling up.

Boss Chick eased up the pressure, manipulating her grip on him, winching. She tightened again as she rose upwards. "Did a bitch have her mouth on your dick?" she asked in a mean tone.

"Never that." All Con wanted is her right now. "What's up with all these questions like I'm on trial in court, baby?"

Boss Chick lowered her hips, rocking slowly sensually. "That's too bad," she said as she tightened once more. She sped up her pace, turning their love making into passionate fucking. as sweat glistened on her body. It had been too long for them both. "If you would have said yes, I would have told you to let me watch the scene," she whispered in his ear.

Con roared like a lion in a den and his whole entire body tensed as he released himself inside of a woman he loved with all his heart. Boss Chick kept her pace despite the fact that she was spent. She was too close to her own orgasm to stop now. Con sat up and reached around her body to thumb her clit. The friction of his hand was all it took. He long stroked her swollen knob until it pulsated. Her back arched up like a cat feeling threatened. Her head flew back as he grabbed her, then her breast. "Give it to me, baby," he whispered in her ear. Boss Chick rained all over his dick and her body went limp as she leaned against him. Con's manhood went limp and easily retreated out of her as he pulled her backwards until she lay beside him against the sweaty silk sheets.

"How did you know where to find me?" Con asked.

"You failed to come home that night with that bitch. To be honest, I'm resourceful when a bitch need to be," she said as she stared at the wall as they spooned, while he ran his fingers through her hair. "Con, baby, I used to hurt and kill them, a living. Finding your love wasn't that hard."

The sound of police sirens broke through the silent night and Con looked around in confusion. It turned his attention to his security cameras. "The police are here outside," Con announced. Unmarked black cars were pulling onto their property.

"They must've found out about Karen and Thug's bodies," she whispered as she rushed through the house in her robe. Her feet slapped the cold tile floor as she walked toward the front door frantically. She flung open the door and ran out into the yard, meeting the officers in front of Con's home before they even got out of their vehicles. She was taken aback when she saw how many cop cars were outside. By the time she realized something was wrong, it was too late. Twenty-seven federal agents and many local police department agents exited their vehicles swiftly with automatic weapons aimed toward her face. Red beams appeared all over her upper torso. Boss Chick looked down and she realized that all it took was an itchy trigger to end her life.

"Let me see your hands! On the ground now!"

She went deaf as the thunderous hum of a helicopter roared above her head. The windstorm that it created as it circled above her, shining a bright spotlight on her, caused her to blow.

"What? What's going on?" she shouted frantically.

"Hands up, now! On the fucking ground now!" She was manhandled to the cement ground as she resisted their demands. She watched as the police swarmed Con's home. "Wait!" she screamed as she tried to stand and give Con time to exit the home through the underground basement.

One of the policemen put a forceful knee in her back, causing her to grimace in pain as he cuffed her wrists. The metal bit into her skin and her wrists snapped from the agent's back force. They held no sympathy for her as they made their arrest.

"You can't do this to me! I've have done nothing wrong!" She had no idea why she was even under arrest, but the feds came at her so heavy that she could assume the worst. Her heart broke in half as she looked out of the rearview window and tears rolled down her face. She realized that the feds got involved and it's a new game when they step up to the plate. "Please, just tell me what's going on right now?" she asked, as snot and tears wrecked her beautiful face. There was no keeping her composure. She was distraught. She knew that the tides of life were changing.

"We will place you in temporary custody at this moment," the officer said as he drove away from Con's home.

"No, please! You can't," she said with a gasp.

"We can do what we want, unless you can tell us something that will make us change our minds and set you free. Your cooperation will make all of this go away. Do yourself a favor and save yourself. It's in your best interest to start talking now!"

"I'm not telling you shit," she stated as she sat with her hands behind her back.

They made it to the feds' hiding spot and took Boss Chick out the vehicle to a little room and started questioning her more about different issues.

"We have evidence against you and Con. We've got you for several charges, including murder."

Boss Chick kept her eyes on the wall in front of her, barely blinking as she blocked out the voice of the federal agent. Growing up in the Daniels Cartel had prepared her for this, "You don't have anything on me, let me go now please."

"We have everything we need on you, mama. You recognize these faces in this picture?" The FBI Agent tossed photos of Thug and Karen onto the table in front of her. She turned pale in the face and her stomach started to turn inside. "Not so cocky now, huh, baby girl? We packed up over twenty-seven directly affiliated with the Daniels Cartel. You standing tall, but do you honestly think all of them will too?

Now, the way this works is whoever talks first gets the best deal. There is only one way out of this, Boss Chick?"

"Damn, you know my street name?"

"Yeah, and there is one way out of this again…"

"What is that?"

He uncuffed her small wrists and told her she was free to leave.

"Thank you, sir, you have a nice day."

Chapter 11

In the heart of the hood two brothers rose from the cracked sidewalk of their impoverished neighborhood, a place where dreams often went to wither. Junebug and Peanut, as they were known in the streets, had seen enough of the desolation and despair that clung to the people around them. They were clever, ambitious, and as life would reveal, unafraid to cross the shadowy lines of morality to craft their own empire.

Junebug, the elder, was a man of stature, with a wiry build and easy smile. He was the charmer, the people's person. Together, they formulated a scheme that would rely on the darkest of trades to accomplish the lightest of ends.

Rising through the ranks of the city's underground, Junebug and Peanut quickly learned the art of the drug trade. They built connections, established routes and before long, their names became whispered in awe and fear in the hidden earners of the global underworld. They were uncannily successful, master minding innovations in distribution and production that not only attracted users but also ensnared those in power who craved control and riches. Their operations spanned continents, with fingers in political pots and law enforcement pockets. They built a cartel! that didn't just rivaled the states, it overshadowed them, becoming an entity that could command economies and dictate to the mightiest of nations.

The brothers, however, had not forgotten their beginnings. As their wealth multiplied and their influence reached dizzying heights, they covertly funneled vast resources back into the "hood" that had raised them. Schools began to appear where once there were none, hospitals and clinics rose from the ashes of broken infrastructure, scholarships and business grants were bestowed to those with a vision but without a means.

All the while, Junebug and Peanut remained phantoms, operating from the shadows to transform their community into an oasis of opportunity within a desert of neglect. The people, unaware of where the windfall originated, began to look to the future with something that had long been in short supply, hope.

Authorities worldwide were baffled by the changes happening in that particular neighborhood. It became a model of urban renewal, a case study for economists and social scientists. All the while, the brothers watched their grand design unfold, veiled from the seating of the work by sublime layers of inscrutable businesses and puppet figureheads. As their power peaked, the brothers knew the risks of their empire's continued growth. There had to be plans in place for a new structure, a system to ensure their legacy without the need for their ominous trade. The cartel had to evolve or be dismantled before it crumbled and took everything they had built with it.

The brothers set their sights on legitimizing their operations. Using their amassed wealth and influence, they slowly transitioned into legal enterprises. They invested in technology, green energy and biotech, becoming pioneers of innovation rather than the underground. Gradually, they reduced their dependence on the narcotics that had been the cornerstone of their empire for many years, dismantling the very foundation of their cartel piece by piece.

As legitimate business magnates, Junebug and Peanut had not worked openly in the daylight. They had transformed from kings of the dark to princes of progress, all while funding and fostering the prosperity of their once needy neighborhood. Time passed, and the story of Junebug and Peanut became an urban legend. A tale of triumph and transformation. The world they hell once held in their philanthropy and vision. Their legacy no longer one of a global drug empire but of a work changed for the better, starting with the streets they called home. The cartel that took over the work had given it back to the hood, and while law enforcement still puzzled over the over the enigma of their origins, the brothers knew they had achieved something monumental.

A true change came from the darkest, providing light to those who needed it most. The brothers would occasionally walk through the hood, their identities unknown to most, and they'd smile secretly at the children playing in the parks and the business owners thriving on clean streets. Junebug and Peanut had become more than just names, they had become symbols of hope, proof that even those from the darkest corners could see the brightest light. Yet to know that Boss Chick is the head of the top of the cartel around right now.

The neon lights of the Velvet Underground nightclub sparkled like stars against the walls. Inside, the music pounded, the drinks flowed, and the patrons danced without a care. This realm of theirs, two small-time hustlers with larger than life reputations. They ruled the club's underbelly, trading in secrets and favors, always looking for the next big score. Tonight wasn't about business as usual. It was electric, charged with energy that warned of a brewing storm. Junebug, a wily operator with quicker mind, felt in his boss. He leaned against the bar, sipping his bourbon, his eyes flickering to the entrance every few minutes.

Peanut, his partner, was a mountain of a man with a gentle voice that belied his towering presence. He made rounds through the crowd, his jovial laugh a beacon in the chaos. Together, they were a odd pair, but an effective duo. Yet as the night wore on, unease settled over Peanut, matching the tension in Junebug's shoulders. It wasn't just the regulars at the Velvet this evening. The air carried whispers of a new player in town, the Long Cartel. Hardened criminals who ruled territories with iron fists and took out anyone who dared cross them. Junebug and Peanut had steered clear, but tonight, fate seemed determined to throw them into the lion's den. The throbbing bass of the club's speakers couldn't drown out the buzz of impending conflict.

Peanut's vigilant gaze caught sight of unfamiliar figures filtering through the crowd. Like predators, they move with purpose their cold eyes searching. "Long Cartel," he mouthed to Junebug from across the room. Junebug downed his drink, nodding at Peanut's signal. He weaved through the dancers, his hand skimming his concealed weapon, a small but deadly pistol he called "Stinger." Peanut positioned himself by the exit a strategic move to ensure they had an escape route. They weren't looking for a fight, but they wouldn't be caught off guard, either. The club's energy shifted as the leader of the Long Cartel, a cruel face they named Aries, entered the scene. His eyes locked onto Junebug, and he approached with a dangerous smile. "Heard you control the underground market here, Junebug," he taunted. "Mighty impressive for such a... petite thing." Peanut tensed up, ready to intervene, but Junebug raised a hand to stop him. "The Velvet's big enough for all. Enjoy," he replied calmly. "No need for territory squabbles."

Aries smile widened. "Oh, we're not here to squabble. We're here to take over." His men fanned out, the clicks of their guns' safeties disengaging as subtle as a scream in the silent tension. In the blink of an eye, the club erupted into chaos. Aries' words were the signal, his men pulling out their guns and pointing them at the crowd. Screams and shouts filled the air as people scrambled for cover.

Junebug acted first, his "Stinger" barking out a sharp retort, hitting one of Aries' goons. Peanut charged, his brute strength a contrast to his usual gentle nature. He wrestled a gun away from another thug, firing back as he shielded the attendees with his massive body. Amidst the strobe lights, and gunfire, the fight became a deadly dance. Junebug ducked and weaved, his aim true. Peanut was an unstoppable force, using his bulk to his advantage, knocking the foes off balance. As bullets sang around them, an unexpected player turned the tide. The club's owner, a shrewd figure known as Madam Velvet, had no love for the Long Cartel. He emerged from the shadows, his own security team in tow. They leveled their guns at Aries' men, a silent declaration that the Velvet Underground was off limits. Junebug and Peanut found themselves fighting alongside Madam Velvet's crew, an uneasy alliance formed in the heat of battle. Aries roared in fury, his plans unraveling in the face of unexpected resistance. The Velvet's dance floor turned into a no man's land, the music a faint memory beneath the cacophony of gunfire and desperate cries. It was a grim ballet, where the dancers fought for survival, and the music was a symphony of destruction.

Aries, realizing the tale had turned, sought to retread and regroup. Junebug spotted him edging toward the back door, a snake slithering away from danger. He wouldn't let him escape because this was personal now. With a sprint fueled by adrenaline, he intercepted Aries, his Stinger aimed at his heart. "It's over, Aries. Your reign ends here!"

Aries sneered, a last attempt at defiance. "You have no idea what you're dealing with, Junebug. "I'll burn this place to the ground before I let you have it." A shot rang out, but it wasn't from Junebug's gun. Peanut had circled around with his own weapon and signaled his men to retreat. The remaining cartel thugs followed, slipping away like shadows as the club's survivors emerged from their hiding spots.

The aftermath was a whirlwind of flashing lights and sirens. The authorities arrived, taking statements and rounding up the few cartel members who had been knocked unconscious during the fray. Madam Velvet had already slipped away, her hand in this night's club events to be plausibly denied. Junebug and Peanut sat on the back of an ambulance, battered but victorious. They looked at each other, a silent conversation passing between them. They'd survived, and they'd held their ground. But at what cost? With the Long Cartel pushing back for now, they knew retaliation was certainty. This was merely the first salve in what promised to be a brutal campaign. As dawn approached, the Velvet Underground stood silent, the debris of the night's events a grim reminder of the violence that had swept through it. Junebug stared at the club's marquee, the flashing lights now subdued and wistful.

"We can't let Aries come back," Peanut said after a long silence. "We need to be ready, and we need allies." Junebug eyes narrowed as he nodded in agreement. This was their city, their territory, and their fight with the Long Cartel was just beginning and Junebug and Peanut were ready. They turned away from the club, the first rays of sunlight creeping across the skyline. Together they stepped into the new day, the future uncertain, but their resolve stronger than ever. The Long Cartel might return, but Junebug and Peanut would be waiting, ready to protect their turf to the very end.

***

In the heart of Blytheville, Arkansas, with the mellow strains of a saxophone wafting through a smoky club, a tale of deception and betrayal began to unfold. Jazz was the epitome of cool, a charismatic figure with broad shoulders silhouetted against moody light, a musician whose fingers danced deftly over the keys of her piano. The regular patrons of the Blue Note whispered of her prowess, not only in music, but in matters that stretched beyond the velvet curtains of the club. Unknown to them, Jazz wasn't just dazzling audiences with her melodies, she was working for the feds, serving up information on the city's criminal underbelly.

Ebony, on the other hand, was as mysterious as she was captivating. A woman who ran her business with an iron fist, Ebony's reputation proceeded her. People knew better than to cross her, and yet, with a flash of her beguiling smile, she could persuade anyone to dance to her tune. Ebony was royalty among outlaws, the queen bee in a hive of nefarious activities that spread like tendrils of a shadowy vine, through the entire city. Little did Ebony know that her close confidante, Jazz, had once betrayed her, all those years ago. A betrayal that led to an interlude behind bars, an intermission in Ebony's reign that she neither expected nor forgave.

Time had passed and so had secrets. Jazz, freed from her past but bound by a conscience marred by years of murky undertaking, had settled into a seemingly innocuous role at the Blue Note. She yearned for redemption and a quiet ending to her symphony of a life. However, her past caught up with her like a frenetic be-bop tempo she could not shake off. The feds, armed with files of dirty names and unsolved cases, had knocked on her door one humid evening. They reminded Jazz of her previous cooperation with the authorities and coerced her with promises of protection and a fresh start. They wanted something bigger than the cartels. A network so intricate and perilous, it had managed to slip through the fingers of law enforcement time and time again. Jazz agreed, albeit with a trembling heart that drummed louder than her bassist's solos, to a wire and play the most dangerous gig of her life.

Ebony emerged from prison as a storm cloud, menacing and unpredictable. She wove back into the tapestry of the underground world with a renewed vigor for control. Her network was a whispered legend and her grudges, like her business, knew no forgiveness. Jazz had not been honest with Ebony when their eyes met again, under the fluorescent lights of institutional hallways, under the guise of friendship rekindled. Ebony, with eyes that cut sharper than any blade, hoc simply said, "The post is a ghost, Jazz. Let it haunt someone else." And in those words, Jazz had chosen to see clemency. For a while, their relationship played out like an intricate dance, an undulation of trust and skepticism, expertly choreographed by the heart of past misdeeds.

The Blue Note became more than a jazz club. It was the front for a clandestine operation, a stage where every note played was laced with silent confessions. Jazz's wire was her lifeline, a delicate strand of truth in a web of lies, that filled the ears of the law with every incriminating word. spoken in the shadows. The club was abuzz with the usual suspects, in the low level grunts, silver tongued middlemen, and most importantly, the fleeting shadows of cartel messengers who flitted in and out like phantoms. Jazz performed each night, her melodies a cover for her true intentions, her soft tunes echoing along dark corridors where deals were whispered and fates sealed. With every chord she played, Jazz knew she was strumming closer to her doom. But the music also gave her a sense of bravery. In its rhythms, she found a courage she never knew she had, courage that drove her to believe she could somehow dismantle the empire that Ebony had built, brick by illicit brick.

It was in the back room, among the haze of cigar smoke and the clink of ice against glass, that Jazz's loyalties were tested and her nerves stretched taut as piano wire. The intel she gathered was invaluable. Shipments, rendezvous, names that had only been murmurs before now were brazenly spoken amidst the din. She relayed everything back to the feds, her heart pounding with the intensity of a congo drum. Ebony, however, was not a woman, easily played. She sensed that the songs had changed, the music wasn't easily played just in the keys, it was in the eyes, the shifting glances, the unsaid. She started to put her pieces together, like notes in a complex scale, mapping out the likelihood of a traitor in her midst.

The operation reached its crescendo when the feds gave Jazz the signal that it was time to tighten the noose. A big deal was about to go down, bigger than anything they had seen before, and Jazz was to be in the heart of it, the centerpiece of the sting. Word had gotten out about a meeting, a summit of kingpins, a gathering of cartels under one roof. They would be vulnerable, open to the poised strike of law enforcement, all because of the intelligence that JAZZ had provided. Her mission was clear. Get concrete evidence and get out before she became a casualty of the crossfire.

The night was set, the stage prepared, but so too was Ebony's trap. Ebony had been proactive, disseminating information, watching the reactions as she played her hand like a royal flush. Jazz, unaware of the tightening circle, focused on her task, her mind a medley of discordant thoughts, her task, her mind a medley of discordant thoughts, her silent rhythm in her veins. But Jazz wasn't the only one with a secret. Ebony knew of her betrayal, not through confession, but observation. A telltale hesitation, a faltered step, a lingering finger on the piano that betrayed a heart out of sync. Ebony orchestrated her counter move with the precision of a conductor. On the night of the faux meeting, as Jazz relayed false intel, she found herself ensnared, a pawn in a game of duplicitous chess.

The climax was not a swan song, it was a requiem. Jazz, adorned with her concealed wire, sat at her piano, her audience a blend of nefarious faces. As law enforcement prepared to storm the club, something far more sinister unfolded. Against the backdrop of her own melody, Jazz's eyes met with Ebony's and in that moment, she knew her life's final act was upon her. With a subtle nod, Ebony signaled her men. The wire was discovered, wordless accusations hanging thick in the air. There was no need for a trial, the verdict was passed with the swiftness of shadow falling upon light.

The sirens wailed mournfully in the distance, crescending as they approached, but they were too late. The sting was a disaster, the cartels had been tipped off, the rats had found other holes to scurry into. The Blue Note became a crime scene, a tragedy enclosed within its four walls. Jazz lay motionless on the ground, her blood a dark crimson against the polished floor, her fingers still, her music hushed forever. She had sought redemption, but found a requiem instead, a requiem played out in the key of treachery and violence. The feds arrived to a scene of chaos, to a mission failed and a source silenced. Ebony vanished into the night, her empire intact, her secrets safe. And Jazz? Jazz become a legend, a tale to be whispered beneath the mourning saxophone waits, a stark reminder of the price of betrayal and the cost of justice in a world where the line between loyalty and deception is as blurred as the smoky air in a once lively jazz club.

Chapter 12

Sister Mary pulled Mustafa's shirt over his head and pushed him into the wall. Her lips were pressed against his swiftly, kissing, licking, and sucking. She moaned into his mouth.

Mustafa's hands slid over her hips, around and back, until he was cuffing her ass. The cheeks were soft and warm. "I been thinking about this pussy all day, Sister Mary. When I'm feeling like I'm feeling, you the only one that can take me away from this shit. I need you." He sucked on her neck and bit into it with his sharp teeth.

Sister Mary purred and humped into him. She took a step back and dropped her Gucci robe completely. She grabbed the remote control from the lower dresser and activated the music. Mary J. Blige's "Real Love" resonated from the speakers. She stepped up on to the bed and stood in the center of it, then looked into his cute green eyes and smiled. "I need you too, Mustafa. You know you got this pussy on lock right now." Her body began to move to the beat of the melody. Slowly, her hips started to wind like a snake in the grass. She turned around and showcased the fact that her G-string separated her dark brown cheeks, before turning all the way back around and facing him. Her small hand ran over her stomach, all the way down to her sexy lips. She played over them through the thin, transparent material. "You want me, daddy? Huh?"

Mustafa had already undressed down to his boxers. His dick was rock hard. He was smiling like he won the lottery at a local store. His dick throbbed, jerking time and again. His eyes devoured her body. She was thick, the sexiest shade of chocolate in the world, he believed and from experience, he knew that she tasted just as sweet. He felt some type of way when it came to their relationship because it was the only secret that had ever been kept from church. People in the church house knew. Local player around town. His only wishes were that he stayed away from Sister Mary's fine ass. Many people in the church community knew how hard Sister Mary loved someone and didn't want her to get caught up with a player like Mustafa in the midst. They told Mustafa time and time again after Sister Mary had expressed her like of Mustafa that they never wanted Mustafa to cross those lines, and he had agreed. But over a period of time, she became finer and finer, and thicker. She was an Asian Black goddess. His infatuation of her had risen through the roof, and five summers ago, they started to creep around.

Mustafa nodded his head up at her. "Hell yeah, big boy ready, baby girl. I'm ready right now. Come here now!"

She stepped to the edge of the bed. He reached up and rubbed the front of her panties. The lips were plump. The fabric seemed moist. He licked the juices off his fingers, looking into her beautiful eyes. She opened her thighs a little further and grabbed the back of his head. She thrust her mound into his face. "Eat this pussy for me, daddy. Taste me," she moaned out loud.

Mustafa licked the fabric that encased her wet box. He placed his nose right on her fold and sniffed her chocolate delights. She smelled like strawberries to him, like a shot of pussy that was off limits. He yanked her panties to the side and licked up and down her crease. His tongue invaded her pink, and then he was sucking on her clit that protruded from the top of her hood while two of his fingers slipped inside of her pride and joy.

"Uhhhn! Shit! Shit, Mustafa," she moaned, crouching down just enough to take his thrusting fingers.

Mustafa moved his fingers in and out, faster and faster. Her pussy juices seeped out of her and ran down her thick thighs. Mustafa licked up her spills. He pushed her backward and climbed on the bed like a lion. Then he picked her up and slammed her down fast. He forced her knees to her chest before he was orally making love to her box, sucking and licking all over the folds before focusing on her clitoris. He spread the lips wide and focused solely on her clitoris.

Sister Mary held her pussy open for him. She bucked her eyes as he ate her out with reckless abandon. His tongue was a blur. It sent shivers through her body. Every time he ripped at her bud, she jerked with pleasure. It felt so good that she wanted to tell him how much she loved his fine ass. Instead, she chose to communicate through loud moans. "Mmmm! Mmmm! Mustafa. Daddy... Daddy... Mmmm... Shit. I can't... I can't take it." She arched her back and grabbed ahold of her breasts, squeezing them. The long nipples poked through her fingers.

Mustafa fingered her wet pussy harder and faster. "Cum for me. Cum for big daddy. I wanna taste you more!" Faster and faster, he sucked in her clit as firmly as he could. His tongue went back and forth across it, and then he was sucking again, swallowing her juices.

"Uhhh. Uhhh. I'm cumminng. Oh shit, I'm cumminng!" she hollered before falling back on the bed, shaking as her orgasm rocked her body violently. Mustafa saw her skeet at him. Her pussy spit three times and then began to leak like a broken water faucet. His tongue licked at her secretions. He slurped them and continued to play in her wet pussy. His fingers were slimy wet. He pulled them out and sucked them into his wet mouth.

"Damn, honey. You taste so good to me. You so sweet like candy. You gone give me cavities." She kicked her legs out and pulled him down, flipped him on his back, and pumped his dick in her fist first after removing his boxers.

"Two can play this game." She licked around his dick head and sucked only the tip into her mouth.

Mustafa's eyes rolled into the back of his head. "Shit, babe. That's why I love yo ass not just a Sunday. You something else," he groaned.

She popped his dick out. "I love you too, Mustafa. That goes without saying." She swallowed her spit, sucked him into her mouth and went to work on him. She deep throated him like a veteran in the Navy, adding a bunch of spit to slurp it back up. Then her head was spearing in his lap.

Mustafa whimpered like a chump. He humped into her mouth over and over. His abs tightened. His fingers roamed through her hair while she pleased him. There was something about her that drove him crazy. Whenever he felt alone, he sought her, and the feeling he had of being alone disappeared. He pushed her off him. "Baby, I want some of this pussy. Bring your ass here right now and put that Asian shit on me first, because when it's my turn, we gone fuck like dogs and cats in heat." He laid back and stroked his dick, awaiting her mounting.

She felt her pussy quiver as she took up the position, straddled his waist and reached under her. She took ahold of his long, thick dick. She ran the big head up and down her crease before planting it in her hole and easing down on it. Her eyes rolled into the back of her head as she engulfed him.

He felt the heat and groaned. She was so wet that her cum was already spilling over onto his nuts. It felt like he'd entered into a swampy cave that squeezed him like a fist. "Ride me, baby, Ride me. Now." He gripped her nice ass and dig his long fingers into her flesh.

She arched her back and popped forward. She popped backward and forward again, then repeated the process, taking him deep into her pussy. She leaned down and sucked his neck with her long tongue. "Un! Un! Un! Mustafa, I love you, nigga. Ohh, fuck! Oh fuck, babe. I love you, daddy. Un! Un! Yes! Yes, sir!" Her hips rotated in a circular motion. She rode him faster and faster. "Aw! Aw shit, nigga!"

Mustafa threw his head back and groaned deep within his throat. "Ride this dick like a pony. Fuck me, Sister Mary, the church woman I love so much. Damn, babe!"

She sped up the pace. The bed began to go haywire. The headboard knocking into the wall over and over again. The springs on the bed squeaking. Her shoulder straps fell off her arms, exposing, her nice breasts. Her nipples were so hard that they stood up an inch and half past the areolas.

Mustafa pulled her down enough to suck on her breasts one at a time. He squeezed her pretty breasts together and licked all over them, humping up from the bed to plant his huge dick as far into her pussy it would go. It felt so glorious to him. He felt her tightened her walls and could no longer hold back. "I'm cumminngg, Sister Mary. I'm cumminng, church girl."

She slammed down on his dick, over and over, milking him like a cow. She felt his nut shoot up and tap her walls. She shook and squeezed her eyelids together. The feeling of the invasion was almost too much for her. His warm seed filled her and spilled downward along his length.

Mustafa flipped her over and continued to slowly work his dick in and out of her pussy. It didn't take long before it was hard as a rock again. He threw her thighs over his shoulders and proceeded to plunge into her pussy as hard as he could, fucking that pussy like a beast, while she played with her breasts and moaned with her mouth wide open. He pulled her up by her hair and fucked her hard from the back. Her juicy ass cheeks crashed into his lap. They jiggled, along with her thighs. He watched his big dick go in and out of her pussy. The sight was enough to drive a nigga crazy, prison cell insane. "Damn, this pussy good, baby. This pussy excellent. I'm finna cum again. I'm finna cum again. Ah fuck! Ah fuck!"

She bounced back harder and harder. Her nut was close to the edge. She could feel it. She diddled her clitoris. Pinched it. A ripple went through her and with him. "Uhhh! Shit, nigga! I'm cummin again! cummings, Mustafa," she screamed.

Mustafa came hard and fell on top of her, his dick twitching inside of her. He rolled over and stuck his dick back inside her pussy.

"Ohh, fuck me, big daddy! Fuck my brains out, young nigga!" Sister Mary moaned, feeling his hard dick rammed into her juicy pink pussy while she fucked him in a cowgirl position. She kneeled astride him and leaned forward on her arms, her hands pressed against his bare hairless thick chest while he lay back, giving her full control. Electricity shot through her body. Her pussy began to throb and pulse, getting wetter with each power stroke. His dick was magnetic. Without saying a word, she lowered her breast into his waiting mouth. He rose up a little while still thrusting vigorous strokes into her and started sucking on her fleshy big breast as his hands began to caress her curves all over again.

Mmmm, that's feel good," she cooed, bouncing on top of him. "Don't stop. Oh yeah, feel my tits. Lick them, baby." She leaned deeper into her lover's grasp, folding her body across him. Their gently parted and their tongues found each other. They kissed passionately. He cupped her nice ass as she continued to ride his dick. The fullness of his rock hard dick inside of her tight pussy was a sensory overload, and her legs started shaking.. "I'm fucking cumming, babe! There was moaning, cursing, chanting and groaning. She slid her soft body against him, his black monster dick reiterated roaming every square inch of her pussy. It was absolute pleasure. "I'm cummin," she reiterated loudly.

"Okay."

She froze momentarily. Her G-spot had been hit many times before. And then it happened, her wet pussy started flowing freely as she humped against him. She gripped the bed sheets tightly and held on for dear life, her breathing sparse and her body becoming numb. Spent, she collapsed across his chest. He had given her an earth-shattering orgasm. "So good, babe," she muttered to him.

The two of them lay back down, motionless for a jiffy, savoring the intense feeling. Sister Mary closed her eyes. She enjoyed the comfort of being nestled against a strong man, his arms wrapped around her, their naked black skin entwined. She could feel his heart thrashing inside his chest. He was sweaty. The bedroom had heated up a few degrees.

"I need to open up a damn window." She pulled herself off of him and went toward the window. Mustafa gazed at her fat ass curves for a minute, lost in thought. For her age she still had it going on from head to toe. He didn't realize she was that damn fine until he got her out of her clothes and fucked the dog shit outta her. He can't believe a church woman named Sister Mary is so freaky.

Chapter 13

Boss Chick stepped out the shower naked. She quickly dried herself off with a towel before she exited the bathroom.

She was still pissed that bitches and niggas had the balls to try to make a move on her empire at the club months ago. But what really had her mad was the fact that, that bum ass bitch Mimi had tried to stunt on Boss Chick like Mimi was like that. "Next time I see that bum bitch, I'ma show her something," Boss Chick said to herself as she got dressed. She threw on an expensive, white custom-made female business suit. Every Friday, Boss Chick got her hair done at the same shop, not out of habit, but because Fi, her Spanish hair stylist was the only one that knew how to do her long hair the way she like it.

Boss Chick threw on her shoulder holsters, slid her two .357's down in the holsters, put her blazer over top, and headed out the door. Since Mustafa was in the hospital, nursing his gunshot wound, Boss Chick was forced to use another Muslim security guard named Ali. Ali wasn't as big as Mustafa, but he was definitely a protector and a good bodyguard. Boss Chick, Ali and two other Muslim guards hopped in an all-black Range Rover.

In the parking lot in front of the beauty parlor, Shelia and Connie had been staked out in a hooptie since sunrise. "One of Connie's friends told her where Boss Chick gets her hair done on Fridays," Connie said as she clutched the Tec-9 that rested on her thick leg.

"I hope so," Shelia huffed. He couldn't believe Boss Chick had actually shot somebody in the shoulder. She was out to redeem herself by any means necessary.

"Can you believe how the bitch tried to front on me in the club?" Connie huffed. "If her punk ass security wasn't there, I would have washed her up!" Connie was about to finish her rant until she spotted a black Range Rover creep up in the parking lot. "Be on point, I think this is her right here pulling up," Connie said in a serious tone. Shelia and Connie watched closely as they watched the Range Rover's every move.

Ali pulled up directly in front of the beauty salon and left the engine running as he hopped out, and walked around to the back of the truck, and opened the door for Boss Chick. The other two security guards hopped out the truck, scanning the parking lot as their boss hopped out of the back seat. Boss Chick's heels hit the solid concrete with confidence. She took only five baby steps before she heard gunfire. Immediately, Ali tackled Boss Chick to the ground and covered her with his own body, while her other two security guards had a shootout in broad daylight with the gunman.

Connie aimed her Tec-9 at one of Boss Chick's security guards and squeezed the trigger. The machine gun rattled in her hands as the bullets ripped through the first guard's body effortlessly. The other bodyguard tried to take cover behind the truck, but a bullet grazed his face, causing his body to drop and hit the concrete hard as hell.

"Get the fuck off me!" Boss Chick screamed as she pushed Ali off her. She quickly kicked off her red heels and snatched her two .357's from her holsters, as she crept over to her truck for cover.

"Nah, bitch, don't try to hide now!" Connie yelled as she opened fire on the truck, rocking it back and forth. Boss Chick ducked down as broken glass rained down on top of her head.

"Boss Chick, I'm going to distract them," Ali said with a scared look in his eyes. "You get in the car and take off while I do that."

Boss Chick replied with a head nod. Three seconds later, Ali sprang up from behind the truck, busting his 9mm. He had several handguns with him. Boss Chick quickly hopped in the driver's seat of the car, as she watched the gunmen riddle Ali's belly with bullets. The two gunmen then quickly ran towards the front of Boss Chick's truck and opened fire.

"Shit!" Boss Chick cursed, as she threw the gear in reverse, and stamped on the gas pedal, she ducked down as several bullets exploded through the front windshield. Shelia and Connie walked towards the truck, shot after shot. As it backed up, the truck crashed into something, making a loud bang. Kept her head down and her away out of control. Boss Chick stepped on the gas pedal, until Shelia and Connie reloaded their weapons as they moved closer to the truck. Boss Chick kept her head down until she heard the gunfire stop, she quickly reached down and grabbed her .357s off the floor. "Y'all wanna fuck with a crazy bitch?" she yelled as she opened fire from the inside of her truck.

Boom! Boom! Boom! Boom!

Once she saw the two gunmen scrambling for cover, she quickly hopped out the truck and took off on foot. Boss Chick ran down the street barefoot with a gun in each hand, yelling for help.

Connie was about to chase Boss Chick, until Shelia stopped her in her tracks. "We gotta go!" one of the men said with a tight grip on her shirt. Connie didn't want to hear it, but Shelia was right. If they didn't leave now, they would definitely be seeing the inside of a jail cell for a long period of time.

"Fuck!" Connie cursed loudly out of frustration as she and Shelia ran back to their car and peeled off.

Boss Chick ran out into the middle of the street causing cars to come to a halt. The bottoms of her feet were on fire, but she ignored the pain and kept on sprinting. Boss Chick ran straight to the bathroom.

"Somebody's in here!" A lady yelled when the bathroom door snatched open. The butt of Boss Chick's gun quickly silenced the woman, knocking her out cold. Boss Chick stepped over the woman's body as the wiped her prints off the guns, and she removed the top piece off the back of the toilet in the park's bathroom. She dropped them down in the toilet tank, in the water. She put the lid back on top, then left like nothing ever happened. Boss Chick went outside and made a phone call to someone to come pick her up and told them where she was at the moment.

While Boss Chick waited, the only thing was on her mind were murderous thoughts. Boss Chick couldn't believe that they had tried to take her out in broad daylight, and had her running for her life, bare foot. A situation like this called for desperate measure Boss Chick quickly pulled her phone back out and made a call to one of the most ruthless killers she knew. On the second ring, a raspy voice answered the phone. "Hello?"

"Good evening," he answered.

"Hey, Taco. It's Boss Chick."

"How you been doing?"

"Not too good at the moment. How about yourself? Some new jackers just tried to take a bitch out in broad daylight."

"Broad daylight," Taco echoed.

"Broad daylight," Boss Chick repeated as she hopped in her ride. "Taco, I need you right now!"

"I'll be there first thing in a couple of hours, just have someone to pick up in Memphis at the airport. I'll call later." Taco was the most ruthless hit man out in the streets. He made a name for himself by always going overboard on his targets. Taco and Boss Chick had grown up ten blocks away from each other, before he made a power move and moved to a nearby town with the white folks. Taco knew if Boss Chick called him, it meant business. He smiled as he began to pack several bags. He wasn't sure the niggas were ready for what he was about to bring, but ready or not, he was on his way.

Chapter 14

Two weeks later, Con sat at his crib watching the NBA Playoffs, getting his drink on. In his new life, all he did was stay in the crib most of the time, staying off the police's radar. He didn't really like or enjoy living like this, but he had to do what he had to do. Con was excited that Boss Chick didn't get harmed, and Taco didn't come to help her like he claimed he would. *I'm her man so I'm the nigga to protect her to the fullest, not another nigga.* Con missed living the fast life, and sometimes he found himself thinking about C-Note, back when he was a nobody in the projects. It was C-Note who had given him the opportunity to become a known nigga, and to make some money. Con poured another shot of Henny for himself when he heard a noise coming from by the front door. He quickly grabbed his .40 Glock off the coffee table and headed towards the front door to investigate. When Con reached the dining room and saw who was standing there, he immediately lowered his weapon.

Boss Chick stood in Con's dining room with six of her Muslim bodyguards, with a smile on her face.

"What you doing here?" Con asked as he walked over to give her a hug.

"I need you," Boss Chick said, cutting straight to the chase. "I need a real goon like you on a bitch team, shit getting real out here right now."

Con took a swig from his glass before he replied. "Nah, I'm out the game, I ain't put in no work in mad years, plus you know I'm a wanted man!" He smiled.

"Fuck the police." Boss Chick walked over, helping herself to a drink. "You told me if I ever needed you, all I had to do was holla at you, and right now I need you more than ever."

"I don't know," Con hesitated. He knew what Boss Chick was asking him to do, and he had to admit that the life he was living was the most boring life ever. Truth be told, he missed the action, and more importantly, he missed *her*.

"Some new clowns out here running around thinking they the shit." Boss Chick smiled. "I need you to come show these niggas how it's really done. Taco failed me, but I'm cool."

Con smiled. "Give me a little time to think everything over."

"No, fuck all that! You can get some more this pussy!" Boss Chick spat. "I need to know right now, are you in or not?"

Con sat there for a minute, as he took a few more sips from his glass. "Fuck it, I'm in for life!"

Boss Chick sat sixty thousand down in front of Con's face in a duffle bag. "Go get dressed, we got work to handle, baby." Con picked up the money and examined it for a second before heading upstairs to get the rest of his belongings. Boss Chick sat on the couch enjoying a drink while Con went to get dressed. She knew with Con on her side, a lot of things were going to be different. She needed a live wire on her team again, someone who just don't give a fuck about nothing. To be honest, Con was her man. Besides, he was trained by hood niggas, therefore she knew he could be trusted to go to war.

On the ride back to the spot, Boss Chick told Con all about Melvin and his crew, and how they had her running down the street dodging bullets barefoot. She also told Con about the crazy hit man Taco that was supposed to show up at the time, but he failed to help her.

"I see a lot of shit have changed since I've been gone."

"But I still have several homes around here!" Con said, putting fire to the end of his blunt. "Don't worry once I get you full back, I'll get things back under control," he assured her that.

"These niggas wanna fuck with me?" Boss Chick said out loud. "They're fucking with the right bitch!" For the rest of the ride, Boss Chick brought Con up to point on everything that occurred. When Boss Chick's guards pulled up in front of her huge mansion, they saw a man standing directly in front of the front door. The man wore a pair of True Religion jeans, Gucci boots, and a Gucci button-down shirt. The top two buttons of his shirt were unbuttoned, exposing his chest, along with several diamond chains that rested on top of the taco-meat-looking hairy chest. The man had long hair that came down to his shoulders, and on his face, he sported a rugged looking heard.

"Fuck is this clown in front of your door?" Con asked.

"That's my main man, Taco," Boss Chick said with a smile as she exited the vehicle, heading towards the well-known killer. "Glad you could make it on such a long notice."

"Come on," Taco said, opening his arms for a hug. "You know whenever you call me, I will be there, but sorry it took a minute or two."

"Taco, right here is my dude, Con. Con, meet Taco," she introduced the two. Con and Taco shook hands quickly before all three of them went inside. Boss Chick led them through the crib, and into her business office.

"So, who are those men that's been giving you so much trouble?" Taco asked in broken English.

"Some faggot nigga named Melvin," Boss Chick huffed as she handed him a folder with pictures of Melvin and all the top members in his cartel organization. "I need you to hunt each and every one of those bitches down and kill em!"

"My pleasure," Taco replied as he studied the folder.

"What you need me to handle?" Con asked.

"I just need you to hold me down," Boss Chick told him. You going to be kind of like my bodyguard... where I go... you go!"

"I got you, babe," Con said. In his mind, he felt this would be the easiest job he ever had.

"While Taco is taking care of that," Boss Chick said, looking over at Con, "I got something for you to take care of." She smiled.

***

Connie moaned passionately as she wrapped her legs around Vimp's head. "Don't stop, baby!" She continued to moan, thrusting her hips up and down, grinding her pussy on his face until she finally came. He then slid in between Connie's legs as he slipped right inside of her pussy. He pinned her legs back to her shoulders and plunged in and out of her walls at a fast pace until he exploded. Once the two were done, Connie ran to the bathroom and took a quick hot shower.

"Get dressed, we gotta get going," Connie said, lotioning her soft body up.

"What's the rush, babe?" Vimp asked, laying across the bed naked with his eyes closed.

"Cause Melvin supposed to be having this meeting down at the warehouse," Connie reminded him.

"Shit," Vimp huffed. "I hope this ain't no meeting about that bitch Boss Chick. I'm tired of hearing about that hoe around here."

"The faster we kill that bitch, the faster all this shit will be over with," Connie said, loading her 9mm. Connie hated

Boss Chick and couldn't wait until the next time they crossed each other's paths. She looked forward to the challenge.

One hour later, Connie pulled up in front of the warehouse and saw goons standing out front. After greeting each soldier, Melvin got everyone's attention. "We at war right now," he began. "This bitch Boss Chick thinks she can hang with the big boys, so we gon' show her what time it is. I don't care where any of you run into her at, I want shots on sight," Melvin said, making sure he made that part clear. Just as Melvin was about to continue his long speech, he saw a white Lexus cruising down the block at a slow pace, blasting Rick Ross music.

Con cruised by with one of his chicks in the front seat, and three of his shooters in the backseat. "Look at these niggas," he smized as he grilled each man as the vehicle went past.

"Ain't that one of Aries' boys?" Shelia asked, eyeing the car.

Melvin pulled a .45 handgun from his waistband and fired three shots at the car. He wasn't sure who the driver of the car was, but he didn't like how they drove past grilling him and his crew. If it was one of Boss Chick's workers, he wanted to let them know what time it was.

Con stomped on the brakes after he heard the three shots ring out. He and his crew hopped out of the car and opened fire on Melvin's crew. Melvin and his members returned fire, holding court in the middle of the hood. Con and his crew hopped back in the car and peeled off. They were outnumbered and outgunned. "Don't worry, we gone catch them niggas again," Con said as he hopped on the ramp, heading to the highway.

Chapter 15

Three hours later, Melvin sat over by the bar area in his crib having a strong drink. Ever since he and Boss Chick had been beefing, he'd noticed that his money began to slow down a bit due to all the heat from the laws. In one ear, he heard his father telling him it wasn't good for business, in the other ear were his goons, telling him to let them go out and hunt Boss Chick.

"I'm telling you," Mike said, having a seat next to him. "Your pockets are going to be the only ones hurting until this stupid war is over."

"Listen, I know that's your new girlfriend and all, no disrespect, but I don't know that bitch. So don't speak about none of my business in front of her," he said, looking over at Trina who sat on the couch.

Trina didn't like Melvin. He looked at her and treated her as if she was an undercover cop or as if she was wearing a wire. This was the sixth time the two were in each other's company and each time, he'd treated her like an outsider.

Melvin knew Trina was his pops' new girlfriend, but for some reason he didn't like or trust the bitch. Truth be told, he really didn't even want her in his crib, but since she came with his daddy, he allowed her inside. As everyone sat around having drinks, Melvin heard his doorbell ring. He looked over at his camera and saw a monster and what looked like three guards with him. "Let that nigga in," Melvin yelled over his shoulder.

The monster stormed inside the house with a nervous look on his face, like he had just seen a ghost.

"What's up, player?" Melvin smiled, looking the monster up and down. After just one glance he could tell that something wasn't right. "What's wrong with you?"

"That bitch Boss Chick," he started off, grabbing a bottle of water and taking a swig. "The bitch came up to my gym with like twenty of her henchmen, flashing guns all over the place," he paused to take another sip of water. "Come up in there talking about I better take a dive in my next fight or shootout, or else she's going to have me killed on the spot."

"Damn, my nigga, you look shook." Connie laughed.

"Nah, this ain't no game to play, this bitch is for real," he told them. "She even shot one of my homies."

"This shit is going too far," Mike said as he sent Trina out into the sitting area so she couldn't hear anything that was being said.

"Fuck that bitch." Melvin downed his shot in one gulp. "I got too much cash riding on this shit for me to sit back."

"So, what the hell am I supposed to do if this crazy bitch storms into my spot again?" the monster huffed.

"Calm down." Melvin stood up. "I'll have a few of my men hold you down."

"This shit ain't no joke," the monster continued his rant. "My mind needs to be clear while I'm out here or else nobody won't be getting money."

"I'll take care of it," Melvin said, looking over at one of his goons. "Have a few of your best soldiers hold this nigga down wherever he goes."

"This is the challenge of my lifetime to win!"

"I got you player?" Melvin said as he answered his ringing cell phone. "Who the fuck is this?" he asked.

"Hey, Melvin, it's Boss Chick. Sorry for calling you so damn late," she apologized.

"It's no problem. You know I don't sleep when it's war time, what did I do to deserve a nice phone call from you, queen?"

"I hate to bother you, but I kind of need a big favor," Boss Chick said.

"Anything… you name it," Melvin sensed that something was wrong for her to be calling him so late.

"I really don't want to talk over the phone. Is it possible that you can come over to my crib please?"

Melvin flicked his big wrist, glanced at his shining Rolex that read 1:45 AM. "I'm on my way, baby girl. I'll be there in thirty minutes," he said, ending the phone call. "Come take a ride with me real quick," he said to one of his niggas as they stormed out the front door into the car.

***

Boss Chick sat at her round table, looking at her three main goons.

The three of them had been coming up with a perfect plan to get rid of Melvin, and his cartel. Boss Chick felt that Melvin wasn't on her level and wanted to make an example out of him. "It's been two long hours and he hasn't come yet," she mentioned to her crew.

"Boss Chick and a few of her home girls bumped into him and his whole army the other night," Con said. "Dumped on them niggas in their own hood," he boasted.

"Just because we at war, we still have to stay for the workers, and make sure the money keeps running in," Boss Chick reminded everyone at the meeting. "All I need you three to do is hold me down and keep these goons off my ass," she laughed, joking around.

"That won't be a problem," Con said with a smile. He lived to put in work, action excited him. Any chance he got to act a fool, he took full advantage of it.

"I have a feeling them niggas are about to try to make a power move on us, so be on point."

Boss Chick poured them all another shot when she noticed a lot of movement in her surveillance monitors. "What the fuck is this?" she said with a confused look on her face as she watched several cop cars swarm the front of her spot. "Look at all these bitches." She tapped Talley to get his attention.

"We banging out?" Blast asked, ready for whatever. Prison was a place where she couldn't see herself being, she'd rather be dead, than locked in a cell twenty-four hours a day.

"No, let's see how this plays out first." Boss Chick smiled. "If anything, we'll be out by the afternoon– I meant morning."

Three of her guards came running in. "The cops are here." He was holding a loaded .45 handgun pistol in each hand.

"Stand down," Boss Chick announced to her whole team. The last thing she wanted right now was a shootout with the police. All of a sudden, the laws busted through the door with a pipe, and it looked like they were ready for war!

"Get on the floor now!" they all yelled about the same time.

"I'm not doing shit until I see a damn warrant around this bitch," Boss Chick said, finishing her drink.

"Well... well... well..." Detective Snow sang as he entered the mansion with a large piece of paper in his hand. His hazel bottom shoes clacked loudly against the floor. "Sherry, I've heard so much about you," he said, standing directly in front of her. He didn't know her name for sure as you can see. In a swift motion, Snow pulled out his .357 Glock and back-slapped Con across the face without knocking him out cold. "Eyeball me again, nigga!" he yelled, looking down at Blast and Telley. Detective Snow slid his weapon back down into his holster and then gave Boss Chick his undivided attention. "Word on the street is you've been making a lot of cash around here," he laughed. I want some of that dope money!"

"I don't know what you talking about," Boss Chick replied. "You must got me mixed up with some more niggas or bitches."

"Oh, really?" Detective Snow laughed as he pinched Boss Chick on the side of her body, causing her to drop down to her knees. "I'm not the one you want bullshit with." He grabbed her hair, forcing her to look at him. "You will break me off thirty-five percent of what you bring in, or I'll make your life a living hell from now on!" He tossed her back down to the hard floor and shoved his knee down on her neck as he cuffed her up. They began searching the mansion. An hour later, they found forty handguns, two duffle bags of cocaine, and six duffle bags full of cash.

"Why do you have all this shit in here?" Snow asked her with his famous grin on his face. Boss Chick knew Snow was fishing for information. She'd been in the drug game for many years and knew the slick shit that comes with it.

"You must don't know who I am around here?"

"I don't give a fuck!" He turned and back slapped her across her face like she was a bitch in a strip club that refused to dance for her pimp. He then roughly shoved her in the backseat. "After spending a few nights in jail, maybe you'll see that in my work, you're powerless," he said, slamming the door shut. Boss Chick didn't know who this detective was, but one thing she knew was he wouldn't be breathing for much longer around here. She was the Boss Chick that had everything a bitch wanted in life, and shit hit the fan that fast. *Who could have told the laws on me and Con?* she thought.

***

Today, it was three months later, and it rippled with a difference. A lawyer was coming in to speak with Boss

Chick, a pro bono lawyer to review her case. Boss Chick's eyebrows knit with curiosity, her thoughts whirling. *What new legal technicality had surfaced? Could this visitor alter my fate?* The door clicked open, and in strode a man with a presence that belied the humble surroundings. His suit was immaculate, his stride sure. With a polite nod, he introduced himself as Mr. Rafael Serrano. His voice smooth, his words precise. They carried a weight that commanded attention yet paradoxically soothed. Boss Chick found herself oddly compelled to trust him, which rattled her current predicament.

As Rafael unfolded her case files, his eyes fixed on hers. I've reviewed your situation," he began, his tone a blend of sympathy and business. "I believe there are avenues yet an explored that could reduce your sentence, perhaps even secure your release."

She blinked, hope fluttering in her chest like a caged bird. "How?" she asked, her voice barely above a whisper.

Rafael's glance flickered, a shadow passing over his otherwise impervious demeanor. "There were irregularities in how the evidence was obtained, and in the conduct of your trial. I plan on exploiting these to file for an appeal on your behalf."

Hours stretched as they poured through the details. Rafael's legal acumen was undeniable. He navigated through statutes and precedents with the ease of a seasoned mariner charting a well-known sea. As the meeting neared its end, a guard announced that visiting hours were over. Rafael rose, closing his briefcase with a click that rang out like a period at the end of their momentous conversation. But before exiting, he leaned in close enough that Boss Chick could catch a whiff of his expensive cologne mingling with a scent she recognized but couldn't place. His voice was a low murmur. "I have a vested interest in you. We have more in common than you might think." He left her with that cryptic parting shot, puzzling her tired mind.

Weeks turned into months, and she noticed the change in tone during her legal hearing. Rafaels tactics were working. There was talk of a retrial and arguments over the legality lack of evidence. Yet, his final words continued to haunt her. What connection could they share, beyond attorney and client? The truth emerged in a twisted revelation months later, when a rival cartel was taken down. Among the evidence served was a ledger, and in it was a detailed account of sanctions and codes. His facade of a legitimate lawyer belying his true identity, a drug kingpin who, unknown to her, had been subtly orchestrating from the shadows.

In a dizzying moment, the pieces locked into place. His emergence wasn't coincidence or altruism, it was a calculated move. She wasn't just a random inmate. She had been selling his product. By securing her release, he'd eliminate a weak link in his chain and maintain the facade of an upstanding attorney. The news rippled through the prison, reaching her the freedom on a technicality. As she walked free, relief and bitterness, intertwining in her heart, she knew that her life outside the bars would be forever shadowed by the realization of Rafael's power and reach. Fate had given her a second chance at life, but the cost of freedom came with the knowledge that justice was a matter of influence, rather than truth leaving a silent promise etched within her soul that she would never again fall victim to any grand puppeteer's scheme.

***

Sister Mary pulled up to a local store and waited for it to close. She sat in her Audi until the owner came out with a black duffle bag. She saw the nigga and it was Big Face, the nigga that owed her twenty grand. She'd been dealing with this nigga since she started hustling and that nigga had never been short when it came to paid her. It'd been almost a month since she gave him a package. He thought she had forgotten about the money, but boy was he in for a surprise. She waited in the cut as he closed the corner store. It was dark and she wore dark clothes with a hat pulled down low over her face. When he turned around, he spotted her, and as soon as he did, the nigga took off running down the street. She pulled her silencer out, then shot him in the stomach. When he made an attempt to keep running, she shot him twice in the leg.

"Awww, fuck!" he screamed out. She walked up to him and dragged him like a dead animal.

"Where is my damn money at, bitch nigga?"

"Come on. All of this over twenty grand? We are better than this. We been partners since I started to church with you," he said.

"Fuck that shit. We did business together. Now, where my money at? Your funeral is around the corner, fuck nigga. What you think, word wasn't going to get back to Sister Mary? This my city, nigga, not Boss Chick's. You been gambling with house money, playing childish games."

"That's a damn lie." She heard someone walking and she hurriedly shot Big Face between the eyes and in the head. She dragged his body behind the big dumpster and waited until the person walked past the long dark alley. She peeked around the corner and the coast was clear. She got inside her car and pulled off real fast.

Sister Mary dialed Mustafa's phone number. His number was still the same, and after the third ring, his voice came through the phone. She didn't say anything because she just wanted to hear his voice.

"Hello! Hello!" he answered. Sister Mary sat quietly on the phone for a minute and didn't hang up.

"Where are you, Sister Mary?" Mustafa asked her and her heart fell down to her stomach. *We are really connected, Mustafa. It is him, even though he's supposed to be dead,* she thought about Mustafa's baby.

"Where the fuck are you, babe? Do you think this shit is a game? You want to call my phone like some crazy ass serial killer? This ain't the time," he said, then he calmed down.

"Why you doing this? Is that not my baby you pregnant with? Did you go back to church since I've been gone?"

Sister Mary hung the phone up.

Mustafa stared at his phone and thought for a short minute and stated to himself, "I lost my damn mind around this." Mustafa had a strong feeling that was Sister Mary and others playing childish games with him. Mustafa got down on the floor in his bedroom and started doing sit-ups to burn off some steam. Afterward, Mustafa headed to the shower. Once he was done, Mustafa jumped into bed naked. The bedroom door opened without him noticing that Sister Mary was already in the house in the bedroom with a short skirt on. Mustafa played like he was asleep.

"Baby, wake up," Sister Mary said to him.

"Chill out, babe." He rolled over like a baby.

"Mustafa, I want you deep inside me, baby," she said lustfully. Sister Mary got undressed and climbed on top of Mustafa naked. Her stomach was round and full like a basketball. Her breasts were swollen, and her nipples stood out like Russian missiles. Mustafa sat up and took her hardened nipple in his mouth. Her moans filled the room as her pussy dripped on him. His tongue traveled up to her neck and along her chin. Mustafa reached down to his hardened dick and slowly pushed it inside of her. Her light walls gripped him as he went deeper inside her. A painful moan slipped from her pretty lips as she took all of his dick inside her pussy. Mustafa wrapped his arms around her as she bounced down on his big dick. When she parted her legs further, he brushed his thumb across her big clit.

"Yes, baby!" she screamed as Mustafa drilled into her more and more. He sucked her nipples harder and her body trembled. She dug her nails into his shoulders as her pussy busted onto his dick. He plunged further inside, her, digging his fingers into her hips to make sure she wasn't going anywhere.

"What other nigga can fuck a church woman like this?" he whispered in her ears as he jabbed at her spot.

"Nobody, big daddy!" she screamed out loud.

Mustafa pulled out of her pussy before he rolled her over on her back. He pinned her knees against the headboard, his hands gripped her thick thighs as his tongue plunged inside her.

"Oh, oh, oh, fuck!" she moaned. Mustafa pulled her clit into his mouth and sucked on it. After he released her swollen bud, he pressed his tongue flat on her pussy. He pulled her pussy lips together as he sucked her orgasm from her, and she squirted into his mouth. Pre-cum dripped from his dick as the taste of her teased the appetite he had for her juicy pussy... He felt nut drizzling down on his dick. He tossed the covers back and nut was everywhere. His dick was still hard like a brick.

"Fuck!" he groaned out as he jerked himself off while he thought about Sister Mary's tight pussy squeezing his dick as he stretched her open. She jumped on his bed, sniffing around his dick and he hurriedly knocked her off the bed.

"Get back!" he yelled at her and she ran out of his bedroom. He looked at the clock and it was late. He pulled everything off his bed and stuffed it in the washing machine. He took a shower and got dressed real quick. He opened the door to his garage on the west side of town. He revved up his engine and put his helmet on. He decided to take his motorcycle out to cruise through the neighborhood. He took off without a word.

***

Once upon a time, in the gritty heart of the hood, where the buildings wore the facade of neglect and the streets whispered of tough love and hard lives, lived a woman by the name of Felica. She was a beacon of beauty amidst the rough edges of her environment, her eyes were deep pools of hope, reflecting a like that was meant for so much more than the dimly lit avenues and the wall art that told stories of territory and pride.

Felica had built a modest existence within these concrete confines. She worked tirelessly at a local diner, a place where the clink of coffee cups and the sizzle of grease sang a daily tune. It wasn't a glamorous life, but it was honest, and it was hers. During her late shifts, she often gazed out of the foggy windows, dreaming of a world beyond the hood, where the grass was thought to be greener and the sky a clearer shade of blue.

Her dreams, however, weren't solitary. As destiny played its hand, Felica's life intertwined with that of Dante's, a man whose smile could charm the moon from the sky and whose arms promised shelter from a storm. He was woven into the community fabric like the gold threads in an emperor's robe, apparently indispensable, a symbol of elusive success, his pockets always full, though no one knew exactly how. Love struck hard and fast, and in Dante's passionate embrace, Felica felt she had found her fortress. But the fortress was built on pillars of sand. It turned out, Dante's wealth came from pressing powder into pills, the stealthy dealings in dark alleys, and the silent handshakes that transferred more than just pleasantries. In her love-soaked ignorance, Felica overlooked the signs, the late-night comings and goings, the jarring phone calls, the possessive clutch of his pockets.

Their life, however, was splashed with luxury that came from the shadows. Fancy dinners at places where the hood looked like a distant memory, clothes that transformed Felica into a starlet, and a security that was intoxicating. She had reservations, whispers of morality that floated up from the depths of her consciousness, but she hushed them with the rationalization of love and the naïve belief that good intentions could blur the lines of legality. Then came the dusk, when the world as Felica knew it crumble. It was a raid that tore through the fabric of their manufactured paradise. Blue and red lights danced along the walls of their apartment like a discotheque of doom, the thud of heavy boots and the crackle of radios soundtracking the end of their era.

Dante was caught amidst a mountain of evidence, the kingpin of an empire built on addiction and sorrow. The feds had been onto him for months, and in one fell swoop, the charade was over. In the aftermath of Dante's arrest, Felica's life spiraled into disarray. Assets were seized. The diner, their home, the car, the materialistic threads of their outward success torn away. News traveled fast in the hood, and the community's eyes held a myriad of emotions, some sympathetic, others accusatory, as if to say, "She must have known."

Without Dante's income, and with the stain of his actions clinging to her, Felica struggled to find work. Friends retracted into the shadows, unwilling to associate with the downfallen queen of a crumbled empire. Fearing retaliation or perhaps a contagion of her misfortune. Eviction notices appeared like unwanted ghosts at her door, and the savings that hadn't been seized dwindled to nothingness. She was forced to start anew. She left the hood, her shame rendering her nearly unrecognizable. The city's underbelly had transformed her from a hopeful dreamer to a weathered survivor. She bunked on strangers' couches taking odd jobs, selling pussy, from cleaning floors in faceless office buildings to serving at bars where no cared for her name, only her efficient service.

The weight of betrayal and abandonment here down on her, but in the furnace of hardship, Felica found a resilience. she never knew she had. She learned to lean on herself, to find solace in her own company and strength, in her independence. Sleepless nights were spent studying, reading anything she could rebuild, perhaps even help others from falling into the traps that haul ensnared Dante and consequentially, herself.

Years passed, and the woman who emerged on the other side was far from the hood's lost daughter. She had forged her identity, became an advocate for those who were on the fringes, using her voice for the voiceless, her painful experiences a launchpad for a mission of empowerment and change. Felica would never forget the hood, the love she felt for Dante, or the life she once envisioned. Yet, as she stood before crowds, sharing her story of redemption and resilience, Felica realized she hadn't lost everything. She had found something greater within herself, a purpose refined by fire and a spirit that refused to be crushed by the very streets that had raised her.

The city never sleeps they say, but for Felica, sleep seemed like a distant memory. Raised in the distressed heart of East side Lamar, she learned early that to survive, you had to be tougher than the bullet riddled concrete that cradled your dreams each night. After losing both parents to the very streets she called home, Felica was left with a burning desire for power, to seize control of her destiny, and to ensure that no one would ever look down upon her again.

As fate wound its knotty fingers, the opportunity came knocking in the form of a drug war that had been tearing the city asunder. Two cartels clashed over territory and supply, resulting in a chaos that neither the law nor the community could contain. It was the sort of void where someone cunning, determined, and unafraid to get their hands dirty could carve out an empire.

Felica, with her piercing eyes and a mind as sharp as shattered glass, saw the void and wrapped it with her iron will. When the most fearsome shootout erupted at a war chase that served as the main drug cache for the reigning kingpin, she saw her chance. The cacophony was deafening, gunshots ricocheting off coil walls, screams, and the thick stench of blood blanketed the scene. But Felica moved through it all with the grace of the predator she had become. When the bullets finally ran dry, and the smoke began to settle, Felica stood tall amidst the fallen bodies of her enemies! She had rallied a group of loyal followers, young men and women disillusioned by the broken promises of the crumbling society around them. Together, they fought fiercely, cornered and eliminated the competition in a coup that was as deadly as it was decisive.

The aftermath of the shootout rippled through the city's underworld, shaking the very foundations that had long been held by the cartels. Whispers began to spread about the new queen who had usurped the throne through sheer audacity and an iron fisted command over her new soldiers.

Law enforcement was too slow, too tied by bureaucracy and corrupted hands to react in time. Felica capitalized on this flaw, expanding her reach quickly, establishing a network of safe houses, distribution lines, and an unwavering rule of silence among her ranks. Her nickname became Queen from head to toe. She surveyed her empire from the top floor of a derelict building that overlooked her domain She had achieved what many had deemed impossible. But the crown was heavy, wrought with the weight of paranoia and the lives that had been extinguished under the command. Still, she reveled in her power, the control over her destiny that for so long had been denied to her. Yet, as with all hubs of power, rivals saw her ascent as a threat that had to be eliminated. More conflicts loomed, as remnants of old cartels and ambitious newcomers sought to claim the throne from the Queen of Concrete.

She fortified her territory, employed spies, and ingratiated herself with community leaders under the guise of a benefactor Investment in the neighborhoods, parks for the kicks, and scholarships for the gifted masked the gritty underbelly of her reign. It was the perfect camouflage, a queen in sleep's clothing, adored by the public, feared by the underground. But in the shadows lurked a greater threat than she had ever anticipated. The remnants of the old cartel had not been fully eradicated, they had instead fused into a vengeful specter, waiting, watching for the moment when Queen would show a silver of vulnerability. And they found their moment when her closest ally and advisor was found betrayed and brutally beaten within an inch of his life, dangling as a warning at the gates of her territory,

The message was clear, and the Queen was not one to shrink back in fear. She gathered her most trusted lieutenants, strategizing under the cloak of darkness. Her counterstrike a measured spectacle of cunning and violent force, designed to sever the hopes of those who dared challenge her.

The nights echoed once more with the sound of retribution, as Queen and her army waged a silent war that left a trail of unanswered questions and cold bodies behind, ensuring that her reign would remain unchallenged for now. Latoya Jefferson stood on her tower of control, bloodstained yet unbroken. But in the quiet moments of the night, when the city's pulse slowed down just enough, she wondered if the empire she had built was worth the sacrifices made. The queen had won her throne, but the day war shadows could never be outrun. The streetlights flickered below as it to echo her tumultuous reign. However, with steel in her eyes and a firm grip on her kingdom, Queen was prepared to face whatever storms may come for the city, was hers and hers alone or so she thought.

Chapter 16

The cartel wasted no time. They drew first blood. Con had just gotten done with his work for the day at the trap house. As he stepped out of the house, two mini vans pulled up and the side doors, opened up, revealing a team of Italians. They hoped out wielding the cartel's favorite handgun, the Tommy gun. Bullets started flying through the air at such a rapid pace that all Con's workers had a chance to do was get to cover. Three of the men on Con's crew didn't make it. They were gunned down protecting him.

"Give me a handgun or something!" he yelled as they hid behind some of the stone pillars outside of the trap house.

Boss, his head man, tossed him a .40 and Con started doing what he did best, slump shit! He kicked his shoes off and spun from around the pillar and let the .40 state its case. His first two shots found their target. The heavy rounds of the .40 knocked one of the gunmen to the pavement. He ducked back behind the pillar as all the remaining shooters focused their attention on Con. His cartel used this as their chance to mow a few more of them down. One of the bullets from the Tommy guns knocked a piece of the pillar off, slicing Con's cheek.

Fuck!" he yelled, grabbing his face. Con stepped back out, unloading bullets with the shooters. The cartel's shooters were getting outclassed by Con's. He popped out, shot three of them, and ducked back behind a different pillar. Before they realized it, they were down from twenty to two men. Not liking their odds, they retreated back to their vans and sped off. Con ran over to his men that had been hit to see if they were still alive, but they were dead. "Fucking bullshit!" he yelled, bending down to close the eyes of one of his dead guards. Con dialed Boss Chick's number and she answered on the first ring. "Hello."

"Hey, babe!"

"Boss Chick, it's war time! I need you to come now!"

"Wait, slow down a minute. What's going on?"

"The cartel just sent a hit team and they murdered several members of mines." His adrenaline was pumping hard.

"I'm on my way." She hung up the phone. She didn't realize the feds were still watching her at the moment.

Con dialed Tubb's number. Hello!"

"What's up, big homie?"

"This cartel of Aries. We're about to bring this war to their doorstep."

"Say less. Just point the target out and we gon' make somebody family put a black dress on Sunday," Tubb said confidently. "I'm about to call Teresa and we'll be on the highway soon," Tubb told Con what he wanted to hear on the phone.

"Yeah," he answered.

"We about to go to war with Arie's cartel crew, and I need to know right now whose side are you on. Ain't no straddling the fence at this moment."

"Is that really a question?"

"Hell yeah, nigga! Have you forgotten that you were just all cool with Aries, who just so happens to be a Chapo in this world?"

"So?" Con waited for an answer.

"Yo' side, Con," he said, blowing air, through his teeth.

"I need you and yo' team here." He hung up the phone.

"They wanted real war? Well, hey, they'll get that and then some more. Nobody was going to be safe, and that included family members and all."

"That we don't need to meet with everybody and go over no war plans. Most of them would probably just get in war anyways."

"We got you, Con. You stated we were going to bring war to their turf, and that's what we plan to do. Con, you on point."

"How are you gone do that without any help?" Con wondered.

"Handle your business then." Tubb hung up the phone.

Con and Boss Chick stopped at a local store down the block from their destination and got out the vehicle. They went inside the trunk of the stolen Lexus they were rigging in and put on bulletproof vests. Con put on shoulder holsters that held twin .40's in addition to the Heckler and Koch MP-10 submachine gun slung across his chest. Boss Chick was similarly dressed, only her holsters held two .30 Glocks. Con had extra clips for his MAC-11 stuffed in his pockets folded as well as extra ammo for the Glocks.

Con had found out that Aries was a very dangerous man and that he was one in the top five list of the strangest cartels in the world. Con and Boss Chick started plotting that same day to hit Aries. They couldn't find a free moment. "Your mind is gone right now." Con laughed.

"Fuck outta here, nigga." She punched Con in the left arm. "But for real though, I love him, but Cash wants me to move to Chi-Town." Boss Chick dropped a hard bomb on Con. Ever since Con could remember, it had been him and her. When they had nobody, they had each other. Con couldn't imagine running the streets of West Rose without Boss Chick in his corner, ready for war.

"What you gone do?"

Con looked over at her. "Really don't know. I ain't trying to leave you, but. I don't want to lose my baby mother either," he confessed.

"Go ahead down there where she at, nigga. It ain't like you gone be across the world. You just gon' be a few hours away," she said, easing Con's mind. "Now let's get ready to show those cartels motherfuckers what a real war look like!"

As they were pulling into Memphis, Con hit Tubb's cell phone. "Hello."

"What's up, big homie?"

"Why y'all ain't here yet?" Con was playing mind games.

"Excuse me?"

"What's up?"

"We here, but we fittin' to smash out soon from your crib."

"You stated were going to war with the cartel, correct? So me and Boss Chick are about to just to hit Aries, but the time had come!"

It was almost 11:00 PM and Con guessed that Aries was getting ready to lay down for the night. As they crept up to the mansion, Boss Chick heard some growling behind her. She turned around to see a pitbull on her heels.

"Hey, babe," she said, not wanting the dog to raise any alarms by barking. The pitbull came right up to her and started scratching its body.

"Bam! Bam!" An old woman stuck her head out the back door and the dog took off running towards her.

Before the woman knew what hit her, Con pulled his gun out and punched her in the head, knocking her out cold. Con caught her before she could hit the ground. They stepped inside, laying her down on the kitchen floor. *This shit going to be easier than easier than I thought*, Con thought. But he was so wrong.

Boom! Boom! Boom!

Bullets struck the wood paneling above Boss Chick's head. She turned with the Glock .30 and sprayed a quick burst, hitting what they assumed was one of his bodyguards.

Con ran into the front room and put a bullet in the fallen bodyguard's head as he ran past him. Con shot the next bodyguard in the stomach as he came down the hallway.

Boom! Boom! Boom.

A different one came, firing from a different side of the house. Seeing her men on the ground sent Boss Chick into a rage. This shit was crazy because the war started at the front door, then inside the mansion, and now they're everywhere shooting. Boss Chick let her MAC-11 rattle in her hands, mowing down both bodyguards and a third one that come from upstairs.

Con sat up, rubbing his chest. He was a having hard time breathing and his side was on fire.

"Get your shit together!" Boss Chick said, helping Con up off the floor.

"Fuck!" Con winced in pain as he slung his submachine gun up. They went through the entire mansion until they found Aries hiding in a walk-in closet behind his suits.

"Get your bitch ass out here now, nigga," Boss Chick yanked him out, talking shit at the same time. Con had a crazy look on his face. He then FaceTimed Tubb. "Hello!"

"What's up, Con?"

"What you want us to do with this bitch ass nigga, Tubb?" Con showed Tubb they had the cartel head boss.

"Make an example out of Aries, and make sure the whole world knows who did it. The Daniels Cartel forever." Tubb hung up the phone.

Chapter 17

The cartel had called an emergency meeting after Aries' badly burned body was found in his mansion. The couldn't identify his body. They were still looking for his hands, feet and head till this day.

"I tried to tell you guys this was going to be a bad idea and look what happened. The main leader has been killed, mutilated, and dismembered. This is why I said we should find out who we were dealing with. I guess we know now. This shit sounds really scared," Toe Tag said.

"I've lived a full life, so I'm at peace with meeting my God. What about you?" Tat asked, directly his gaze towards other crew members.

"We're past that shit now. The question now is how do we respond?"

"Send goons to kill their whole cartel! It's that simple."

"I don't think it'll be that easy. Now that they know we're trying to kill them, they going to be on point. It's obvious they on a different level than what we thought," Toe Tag said, speaking from the heart.

"So, what's the war plan?" Tat asked. He was one of Aries' right-hand men.

"The game plan is to kill the whole Daniels Cartel family. We just have to figure out how and I need to get the phone because Con had a woman with him when he was going to war with us. If this Boss Chick individual is the same woman, then we're going to need to get rid of her sooner rather than later," Toe Tag said.

"If it's that serious, we can always send more members."

"That's exactly what we need! Should've thought of that myself," Tat said.

Toe Tag sat pondering over the suggestion.

"The next time we meet, it should be about the death of Con and Boss Chick." Tat burst into a laugh.

Now Toe Tag, the new don of the cartel family, they were so focused on this killing of Con and Boss Chick that they had forgotten about the rest of them.

Boss Chick was the typical hoodrat, thick, ain't good for nothing but lying on her back or getting guns in her name, then reporting them stolen. Don't forget about her bad ass kids.

"We about to have some action," Con said as three white Range Rovers pulled up on the scene and popped out. Con wasted no time leveling his .40's their way.

Boom! Boom!

Con's first shots caught one of the men between the eyes, spraying brain matter all over Boss Chick's body. She didn't bother to wipe the blood away with her shirt, but it was too much. Con grabbed his other .45 handguns and went to work.

Boom! Boom! Boom!

Boss Chick was letting her shots fly also, walking toward the Rover truck.

A wave of cartel people came from behind them. When Con and Boss Chick chose to try and kill Toe Tag, they didn't realize that it was a cartel stronghold. Con and Boss Chick were cutting them down with their assault rifles. They were outnumbered and were almost out of ammo. Con was looking out as he and Boss Chick ducked behind a Benz truck in the parking lot.

"We done fucked up," Boss Chick said, looking at Con.

THE PLUG'S RUTHLESS DAUGHTER 3 | TONY DANIELS

"Fuck it! They gone make a movie about us," Con said, standing up and shooting more ammo. Con decided he wasn't going out like a coward! Con and Boss Chick put their backs together and went for what they knew. For everyone that they shot, another bitch would appear.

In the midst of the chaos, Toe Tag had slipped away. Suddenly, five blue Hummers pulled up and a bunch of Mexican soldiers piled out. They immediately went to work on the cartel. The last Hummer pulled up to Con and Boss Chick, and the back window rolled down, revealing Misty.

"Con told me what y'all had going on. I thought I told you that Con was mines," she said as her back window was shattered by a stray bullet. "Get in!"

"You know we had everything under control," Boss Chick said, getting in the back.

Misty raised her brow and looked at Boss Chick, then at Con. "Is this true? Because I can let y'all back out." She smiled.

They both shook their heads no, even though all the cartel shooters were either dead or had been run off. As much as they hated to admit it, they owed Misty their lives because without her and the cartel, they'd have been worm food or bait for the cartel.

Misty knew it too and was going to hold it over their heads in the near future.

***

GiGi was taking a day off from selling days in the city. She was turning out to either be that good or she was just the luckiest bitch alive on earth right now.

Her day was coming. She was sure of that. In the meantime, she was home spending time with her nigga.

"Baby, dinner's ready." GiGi's boyfriend yelled up the steps.

GiGi didn't want to eat because she was on FaceTime with her other boyfriend. She was in love with both of them. The alarm on her phone went off and she noticed her phone was losing connection during the conversation. She hung up the phone and hollered at her boyfriend to come downstairs to see what was going on. Her home alarm was connected to her personal phone. The alarm that had gone off sent a motion sensor in shock and the pit bulls in the backyard were acting crazy. When she looked at the camera on her plane, she saw a lone figure watching the house from the woody area. He threw the dogs some kind of meat inside the gate. GiGi ran to her bedroom, put her vest on, and opened her gun safe. She grabbed her custom-made .45's and a M-4. She was coming back out of her bedroom when the power in the house went out. She took one step at a time, making a move.

She got to the first floor and stood still like a deer seeing a headlight in the darkness. She was in full blindness. She was trying to wait for her generator to start.

"How does it feel for the hunter to become the hunted?" a voice asked from her right.

GiGi bent and fired shots at the person's direction. They had on all-black with a black mask.

"I thought this was the biggest cartel in the world," the masked person said to her.

Boo fired several shots in the same direction of the voice and missed. GiGi had him off his square, both were good until it came to play defense. Then she factored in that he wouldn't be able to get too reckless. She also knew she couldn't afford to play with the masked person, because one slip and she would become the prey real fast.

Boom! Boom!

GiGi shot the person in the chest and arms, knocking the M-4 out of the masked man's hands and spinning the masked person around, but the person didn't fall. The masked person took his mask off and revealed he was Ali, one of the cartel gunmen.

The vest took the brunt of the impact, but he still felt the pain.

GiGi was moving fast when Boo let one of his .40's spit, hitting Ali in the right leg, knocking him against the wall. The bulletproof vest saved him a lot from getting hurt, but not in the leg. Shit was moving fast, and it was a war in the house that shocked the community today. GiGi's aim was on, because the bullet hit Ali in the head, pointblank. GiGi fell back onto the sofa, grabbing her chest. Boo had gotten her on her feet and was about to take another step in a different direction when he raised the .40 Glock back up for war time. GiGi jumped back and fell down as Boo let the .40 Glock talk. The generator came back on, lighting the house up once again.

Fuck!" She continued to grab her chest in pain.

Boo stumbled over to where she was. "Toss your handgun over here, baby." She tossed her handgun to him without a problem. She couldn't believe this shit was happening to her with the man she loved. Now all types of shit was going through her mind about their relationship. Boo tossed his handgun to her small feet. "Now pick it up and hand it to me." When she reached down and grabbed the gun, she handed it back to him. Boo pulled the trigger twice, shooting her in the head and once in the stomach. "Bitch, I knew you was cheating all this time." Boo put the handgun to his head and put his middle finger on the trigger

Knock! Knock!

Someone was at the front door.

Chapter 18

Boss Chick was dressed in all-black, sitting behind the wheel of her big body Benz with Con on the passenger side.

"We gotta disappear again," Con said. He kept his eyes on the warehouse where Toe Tag and his men were stationed at.

Boss Chick looked around the dark rundown black neighborhood, thinking the same shit at the moment. She had to agree with Con, *this shit must go down today.* "Come on. Fuck it, let's get to business," she said, placing a silencer on the tip of her P-85 Ruger pistol. She could've sent a crew to kill Toe Tag but this was personal, and she knew to never send a kid on a grown bitch's mission to cop a nigga head off his body.

Toe Tag was in his private bedroom in the warehouse fucking a stripper bitch.

"Uhm, ugh, yes, daddy," Star yelled. She was throwing her ass back, making it clap, knowing Toe Tag was about to cum anytime.

"Damn, you missed a player," he laughed. He slapped her ass cheeks while giving her deep power strokes and she went ham on his dick.

"Ohh, folk, damn nigga, this dick good!" she screamed at the top of her lungs while grabbing the edge of the bed for dear life, ripping the cotton out. His bitch was going crazy in the bed.

Toe Tag came on her round ass cheeks, she cleaned her cum off of his huge dick by sucking it and making loud slurping sounds while doing her magic with her wet mouth. *This bitch head game was off the scale, like four ounces of soft turning to hard.* "Damn, you trying make a nigga fall in love," he said as he slid his dick in and out of her mouth, all twelve inches of hard dick. "Baby, I need to go back to the meeting where my crew members at. Let me take a quick shower." He pulled his dick from her mouth, before cumming down her long throat.

Star, who was Jamaican, was a lawyer in Blytheville, Arkansas. At thirty years old she had her life together. She was a college graduate owned her own home but was selling pussy on the side for extra money. Her body was nice, and she had several tats on her ass cheeks. Her measurements were 34-28-40, damn she was fine. She threw on her Chanel silk robe and walked in the guest bathroom where Toe Tag was soaking his body. They'd been fucking for a while behind closed doors. She knew that he had been under a great deal of stress lately from the way Toe Tag had been acting. It wasn't the right moment to tell him that she was pregnant by him. She made her way to the hallway to get something to snack on. Since being pregnant, she had been eating a lot. As she reached in the refrigerator, she was unaware of the terror lurking in her rear view. "Damn! Oh my God," was all Star could say when she saw the two masked people with guns pointed at her. "Please, I have a career, I'm begging you for mercy," she pleaded, in tears.

"Where that nigga at?" Boss Chick asked just as she heard the water from the shower running. Star walked down the hallway with two guns trained on her. This was why she wanted Toe Tag to leave the streets alone, because it could harm her like this.

Once in the private bedroom, Toe Tag posted up by the bathroom wall while Boss Chick held Star at gunpoint. "You a pretty woman but the decisions you make within these next few minutes will determine your future, so don't be a superhero at this moment," Boss Chick stated. "Your time has finally come to an end, bitch."

Boom! Boom! Boom!

Boss Chick shot her handgun first and the bullets cut through the silencer and entered Star's thick skull. Then, Con emptied the full clip into Toe Tag's face, leaving their bed sheets bloody. Boss Chick looked back at Con and he had left the bedroom on his way out the warehouse and saw nobody at the table where food was spread all across the table. Boss Chick ran behind him when she noticed Aries' photos on the wall. He was dressed in a Mexican police uniform. There were even pictures with him shaking hands with the head cartel man. Boss Chick had no damn clue that Aries was working with the feds, or even the local law enforcement. Boss Chick caught up with Con at the front entrance and both of them headed out together, holding hands.

***

Sister Mary pulled up across from the warehouse in her white Benz. She killed the engine and lay back in the seat of her Benz, resting her head against the headrest. She closed her eyelids and took a deep breath. This was her way of preparing herself for the murder that she was about to commit. It wasn't going to be for her to lie down at all. And how could it be? Sister Mary was a church woman, like a testament to service and faith. The small parish where she served was her sanctuary, the community, her family. One Sunday, as the church pews fitted and the choir warmed their voices, she noticed a new face among the congregation. Mustafa stood out with deep-set thoughtful eyes. Something about Mustafa struck a chord in her heart, lighting a flame that she earnestly believed was divine in nature.

Over the weeks, Mustafa became a regular at church activities. Sister Mary found herself drawn to his stories of his homeland and his journey to newfound faith. As they volunteered together at the soup kitchen and the homeless shelter, Sister Mary started to see Mustafa not just as a member of the community, but as a kindred spirit. He shared his financial struggles with her, a tale of an earnest man working saving money. Sister Mary believed in helping her fellow man, and she began to extend her generosity toward Mustafa, discreetly offering him money from her own modest saving to ease his burdens.

As the seasons changed, she enjoyed the stolen moments they spent together, whether in silence or shared prayer. There was a part of her that knew her feelings were more than just platonic, and she grappled with the guilt of such emotions. She had pledged herself to God, yet here she was, enamored by a man whose spirit seemed to speak to hers. In her private prayers, she sought guidance and reprieve of these feelings. Yet she could not deny the joy that blossomed within her whenever Mustafa smiled her way.

Mustafa had ambitions of improving his education to support his family better. Finances were a hurdle, so Sister Mary made a fateful decision. Without a word to anyone, she took out a loan against the nuns' convent, rationalizing that investing in one's future was akin to investing in God's plan. She funneled the money to Mustafa disguised as anonymous donations from the church community. Her heart swelled with the generosity of her sacrifices, her singular payment being the light in Mustafa's grateful eyes.

The weight of her decision pressed down on Sister Mary as months passed, and the repayment of the loan loomed. The convent's finances were tight, and she scrambled to make ends meet, keeping her contributions to Mustafa a secret. Meanwhile, Mustafa thrived. His gratitude to the community, to Sister Mary, and to the anonymous benefactor was heartfelt and openly expressed. Sister Mary's heart ached with a mixture of guilt and love, holding onto hope that perhaps one day Mustafa would see her not just as a spiritual sister, but as something more.

Meanwhile, within the walls. of the church, another had taken notice of Mustafa. A young woman named Sophie had been quietly assisting in various church initiatives and had unwittingly become the subject of Mustafa's affections. There were subtle in their exchanges, but there was a warmth between them that Sister Mary hadn't recognized until it was too late.

One evening, after a long day of organizing a charity event, Sister Mary walked in on Mustafa and Sophie in a tender embrace. Her heart stopped, here was Mustafa, his affection and attention entirely focused on someone who was not her. The world seemed to tilt beneath Sister Mary's feet. Every shared moment, every penny given, suddenly felt like the culmination of a grand delusion. She faltered in her steps, grief-stricken, as the truth came crashing down around her. In the days that followed, doubts plagued her. Had Mustafa ever cared for her, or was she merely a means to an end?

Her struggles intensified as she juggled her financial woes and her broken heart.

Mustering every ounce of courage, Sister Mary confronted Mustafa. His shock was genuine, he had never seen her charitable gestures as anything, but selfless acts borne of faith. Sister Mary realized that her feelings, though unnoticed, were never reciprocated. Mustafa's heart was, and had always been, with Sophie. The confession to the Mother Superior that followed was one of the hardest moments of Sister Mary's life. As word spread of her actions, the community's disappointment weighed heavily upon her. The realization that her mission had been tainted by personal longing brought Sister Mary to her knees in penance.

Time, it is said, heals all wounds. Sister Mary's path to redemption was paved with humility and service. She toiled to repay the debts she had accrued and worked to rebuild the trust that had been lost. Mustafa and Sophie moved on, their happiness a bittersweet reminder to Sister Mary of her misplaced love. In the quiet of the church, Sister Mary found her peace, her heart returning to the love that had guided her life from the beginning, her love for God and her community.

"Damn! Damn!" She woke up from her dream and punched and pounded the steering wheel with her fists, accidentally blowing the horn thinking about how Mustafa been unfaithful to her. Afterwards, she opened the door of her Benz and slid out. Slamming the door shut, she took a look around and made her way towards Boss Chick's Range Rover. She found herself at the front passenger door. She knocked on the window and waited for someone to open it. It wasn't long before she heard the locks coming undone and the door being pulled open. Before she knew it, she was standing before her man, Mustafa.

Mustafa was rocking a red Chicago Cubs fitted cap backwards and no shirt, so all his tattooed form was on display. His hands were in a pair of black gloves at the moment. "What's up?" Sister Mary slapped hands with Mustafa and embraced him.

"Nah, I came through because I found out Boss Chick was in the area," Mustafa said, looking at Sister Mary. Mustafa pulled out his cell phone and activated the camera on it. Once he saw that it was filming, he was excited.

"Oh, hell yeah! Where that bitch at?"

"I heard she was here. She probably on West Rose Street."

I got Boss Chick's address," Mustafa said.

They drove from the warehouse and chopped it up about shot, going down in the dope game wars. They made to their destination and headed straight to the kitchen. She grabbed the pot they whipped dope up in and several butcher knives out the kitchen drawer.

Mustafa sniffed something was wrong, because tears slid down his face. With shaking hands, Sister Mary reached into her Chanel purse and grabbed her gun. Mustafa reached to grab her hand but was too slow.

Sister Mary snatched his hand back. Her first connection was his face. She kicked him in his nuts, made him get on his knees and act like a dog and bark.

Blood quickly ran down his face and she didn't pay it any mind because he was caught cheating with another bitch that goes to her church.

"Babe, you going kill me?" He kicked her in the stomach, but she didn't fall. The bulletproof vest Mustafa had on come into play during cartel war, but what about now?

Sister Mary bounced back and slapped him twice with her .40 Glock across his forehead.

"Please don't kill me, baby." He sniffled and more teardrops ran from his eyes. He grabbed a knife off the table and tried to stick Sister Mary in the arm, but she moved to fast.

Sister Mary yanked the knife from him and stuck him in the chest and blood splattered on the marble floor. She tried to stick him again, but her heart would not let her continue.

I'm sorry, baby," he apologized and squeezed his eyelids closed, faking. She turned her head.

She couldn't stand to see the horror etched on Mustafa's face. She dropped the sweeper, and it clanged to the floor. Sobbing aloud, she got down on the floor and pulled Mustafa to her. She looked down at Mustafa's body, his last tear fell from his face as she had thought. He started rocking back and forth, still crying as he held on to Sister Mary.

Having shed his tears and taken a deep breath, the big guy got to his feet and stumbled toward the front door in pain. His forehead feeling the pain from the handgun Sister Mary bitch slapped him with. Mustafa laughed as he headed toward the front door and went outside to his vehicle.

Chapter 19

A month later, Boss Chick pulled up at a local storage building on Main Street. She quickly unlocked it and dragged Con inside. When she hit the lights, Con lost his breath instantly. Inside were five large gun safes of various shades of black, gray and green, that was nothing. What took his breath was the stacked, drab olive green coats stenciled with U.S. Army in pale yellow. Boss Chick immediately opened two of the five safes and pulled out two military grade M-4's, handing one to Con.

She strapped on two leg holsters, then grabbed matching FN-5.7, checked for loads and slipped them into the holsters. And then threw fully automatic Glock 185's, drums, and extra ammo into two large black duffle bags.

Boss Chick was a woman possessed as she knew what was to come. Con had yet to move, being more than impressed by the well-stocked arsenal. Just as well, she knew a lot of people were about to die.

"Boss Chick, you can't do this. I know you're upset, baby."

Boss Chick turned to face him so fast, so aggressively, she staggered.

"Don't call me, baby, or tell me what I can't do."

"Baby, I'm with you till the end."

Boss Chick turned to face him, then stared into his eyes. Giving in, she kissed his full lips and caressed his back, ending with her hands resting on his dick. Instantly his dick hardened just as she became moist. They both were ready until they heard noises from outside which altered their moment of elation. The sound of shuffling and an audible, "Shhh," caused them to be alert. Boss Chick checks her watch, then immediately goes into action. She tossed Con a Level 3 flak vest that he put on, then she put on her own quickly. She dove into the first safe and grabbed a fully automatic MP-5 and tossed a few mags into a bag. Finished, Boss Chick grabbed an RPG and a coat and slung it over her shoulder onto her back.

"Boss Chick, now what? We can't… could be an ambush. We're pinned!"

"Would I be that bitch if I didn't plan this?" She then opened the fourth safe and popped a panel out to reveal a tunnel. "Come on. Just stay to the right."

"How'd you know they'd come?" he asked, impressed.

Boss Chick clicked on the flashlight on the MP-5 sub-machine gun and stepped in. She had yet to enter when she called for him. Boss Chick pressed a series of buttons on the pad of the fifth safe and hurriedly followed Con. After a brisk minute, they came to a dead end when Boss Chick removed a hidden panel. The tunnel had led them to another storage unit that contained a satin black Benz G-63 truck. Reaching under the front wheel, she produced the keys. Tossing the bags in, she directed Con to get in the driver's seat.

"I'm going to open the door, don't go out till I signal you," she instructed.

"Boss Chick, that's a stupid plan. Let's go out on foot first and take out as many as we can. I've got the training, trust me," Con said defiantly.

Relenting, Boss Chick shrugged and stepped out of her way. Stepping out into the night, the moon graced them with enough light to see that the Bentley was blocked in by a van. There were several men standing around, and an untold number inside.

"I see about eight small arms. Unknown number inside, they could have found the tunnel by now."

"'Nah, they didn't find it yet,'" she stated as an explosion rocked them, causing Con to duck and Boss Chick to laugh. "Now they found it." Apparently, she'd rigged it to blow. Those standing outside were now disoriented. That's when the true training kicked in. Unexpectedly, she stepped out with Con on her heels. She clicked the safety off and fired at the first of three men. Giving him and each thereafter double-tap center mass thirty yards away, ending them. The remaining five scrambled for cover. That's when she flicked to fill auto. She sent 9mm rounds into their backs, landing eighty percent of the shots fired.

Con, not hesitating, squeezed his MP-4 and managed to hit one man and sprayed the Bentley on accident. He had enough money and actually cared little about losing the expensive car. A woman was out-shooting him, and he wondered how a simple bitch had the training to handle a fully automatic so skillfully. The last two men fired from behind the bulletproof Bentley. Boss Chick returned fire while she pulled the pin and tossed a grenade, rolling it under the Bentley. When the car exploded, Boss Chick was shielded by Con as it set off a chain reaction. The van exploded as well as part of it, and the coupe rained down across the lot. Once it slowed down, Boss Chick stood in time to see a black Charger speed off.

Knowing Sister's Mary men escaped, and the police were on the way, they raced back to the Benz truck. Boss Chick took the wheel, and it started with a deep growl. She smashed the gas and pushed it out of the storage unit quickly. She took pride in everything she did, so it showed in the upgrades she'd done on this monster. Bulletproofing, upgraded engine, crash bars, and electronics. It even had internal satellite TVs and a refrigerator, and had guns installed in the front and back.

"Baby, where are we going?" Con asked.

"Just ride, baby." She returned a smile and playfully slapped his arm. She thought, *he doesn't know the half of it,* as she pushed the Benz to 100 mph.

Just outside of the city Boss Chick pushed the big Benz's 465 horse powered engine to its limits. Racing to Sister Mary's mansion, her intent was to murder her and whoever stood between them. Con hadn't spoken a word, giving Boss Chick the opportunity to use Google Maps to show the layout of the property. Before he realized it, she pulled into a parking lot and began checking her weapons. She downsized one of her bags and was prepared to go in as if she were Rambo.

Boss Chick knew that if they died, it would be blood shed on both sides. She attempted to put a stop to this cartel war shit. Boss Chick dialed Sister Mary's phone number but got no answer. She got back in the vehicle and started rolling up a blunt. Just then two black GMC vans with tinted windows pulled up across from her. "What the fuck is these niggas doing?" mumbled Boss Chick. Never the one to panic, she reached under her seat for her Glock .40, as Con fired the blunt up that she had just finished rolling up.

"These niggas don't want this action," he said as he choked off the blunt. Con pulled his gun from under his seat and placed it in his jeans and stepped out of the Benz, keeping his eyes on the vans at all times. He saw four masked men, two from each van jump out with AK-47s. Peeping what was going on, Boss Chick already had her Glock aimed and let off six quick shots, hitting two of the gunmen in the head, giving her enough time to jump back in her bulletproof Benz. Con hopped in also on the passenger side, with a sad look on his face. The other two gunmen let out off a volley of shots that bounced off the Benz. Boss Chick hit the pedal and sped out of the area with the vans right behind them.

Con reached in the backseat and grabbed a fully automatic Russian Military special AK-47. The gun had a 100-round drum, and two grenade launchers on the bottom of it. The vans decided to make a left then, leaving Boss Chick by herself. They arrived at Sister Mary's mansion and Boss Chick was excited that it was easy to get at her property and to her front door.

"Uh-um, damn, daddy! I miss that dick," said Caressa, a biracial dime piece, stroking Mustafa's shaft as she attempted to let him take her anally. "Ahhh! Mustafa, slow down, it's too big," Caressa pleaded as she scooted away.

"Bitch, stop moving and handle this muthafucka," demanded Mustafa, giving up and settling for the pussy. He dove into her wetness balls deep on the first stroke, causing Caressa to yell out.

"Where that bitch Sister Mary at? Tell her to get in here. I want both of yawl at the same time." She smiled her long hair was beautiful, but Mustafa didn't care about that he was knee deep inside some good pussy.

"Bitch, I ain't done with you yet! You gone bust it open, or I am." He laughed. "Get that pussy wet and open, baby!" Once he got her wet enough, he entered her pussy giving her inch by inch until his balls finally slapped her pretty clit. Candice walked into the room and joined them without a word. The fuck session become intense because the twins were more than Mustafa could handle alone. Every time he came, the twins ate it up and sucked him back to brick hard. Mustafa refused to have his dick being challenged by the twenty-three-year-old twins. Exhausted, he continued to slam his dick wherever he could. Both of them could've been porn stars, both did anal, both had tight bottomless pussies, and throats with no gag reflex. Their flawless tattooed yellow skin was tight and firm against their flesh. Fresh out of community college, they were still in shape from cheerleading and dancing.

Mustafa was hitting Candice from the back anally as Caressa laid on her back and ate her from beneath. It seemed more like a war as all three of them were covered in sweat. Candice was taking the worst of the punishment from the pounding Mustafa was putting on her, juices squirting and raining all over Caressa's face. Candice was sore as well as exhausted, and could only get a breath between Candice's never ending orgasm.

"Please cum, daddy! Please cum for mama!" she pleaded as she began licking and massaging Mustafa's balls figuring it would be over if he cum one more time. Yes, daddy, put it in my mouth!" said Candice. That got Mustafa, who was just as glad to end it as she was. He pulled out and squeezed his dick so they both could taste him.

"You want this cum, bitches?" He stood up before them, allowing Caressa the first opportunity to swallow him whole. She sucked her sister's juice off him and took him deep. Magically, she teased his balls with her tongue, as she pulled him closer. Candice waited for her turn, while Caressa jumped in position.

"Fuck!" yelled Mustafa as Candice articulated her throat. Mustafa's eyes rolled in the back of his head, as he tried to look up to the heavens, thanking the man upstairs for creating women. In that very instance he came and Caressa, being overly eager, knocked his gun to the floor from the nightstand. He heard the noise but opened his eyes only to find Caressa pulling his wet dick from Candice's throat before passing out, and then pressed her head on to his dick, causing her to gag and tears to roll out her eyes.

Candice then spit Mustafa's cum into Caressa's mouth before they kissed, all the while staring seductively into Mustafa's eyes. "Damn, you bitches got fire head. You earned red bottoms and Fendi bags today. Damn, what else yawl want from a nigga?"

"You just earned a body bag, my nigga," announced Boss Chick as she suddenly stepped into the room followed by Con, strapped with .357s and a single .44 Glock handgun. That's when both of the twins scampered away. Mustafa, realizing his mistake, looked at the twins and thought about going for his handgun. The flaw in that was it was no longer on the nightstand. It was just on the floor, but with three large caliber handguns only feet away, there was no escaping or reaching it.

"Damn Boss Chick, I never thought you'd do me like this," he hollered in a loud voice. As his tears rolled, he whimpered.

"High, I told you," Con screamed out to Mustafa.

Caressa hesitated. "Go bitch," ordered Boss Chick, placing the .357 handgun at Candice's head. "Don't make me do this."

Standing behind Mustafa, Candice pleaded. "Mustafa, please tell them I don't got nothing to do with this shit." She looked at her twin sister Caressa in tears. The moment her hand touched Mustafa's as she dropped a tear, but didn't stop. She got inches closer when the dam broke.

Mustafa felt ashamed about the whole situation. He couldn't believe he got caught fucking with twin sisters in Sister Mary's mansion. He had done all the dumb shit a nigga could do. Now he was in a place that he couldn't get out of and don't know what his next chess move will be.

"Much respect, Mustafa," Boss Chick said, as she personally put two .357 blue talons in the back of Mustafa's head, as blood went everywhere in the bedroom. "Where is Sister Mary at, bitches?"

"Don't know," both of them spoke at the same time.

"Tell her I'm looking for her for a nice surprise gift, she will always remember the rest of her damn life."

"Okay. I will let her know," Candice said in a soft tone of voice. Caressa was quiet as she ran out the bedroom and out the front door with no clothes on. Candice followed right behind her crying loud, with tears rolling down her cheeks.

***

Boss Chick and Con's plan was to storm the mansion with gun blazing. Which was an overall bad idea because Sister

Mary wasn't there. Walking out the mansion, Boss Chick and Con saw Sister Mary sitting in a black SUV, hands wrapped around bundles of cash. It was a brazen display, a statement made with the arrogance of unchecked power, or so it seemed to the enraged Boss Chick. Under the silver glow of the streetlight, Boss Chick breathed slowly, mustering her wrath and strategy into a single command. She raised her hand, a signal undetected by the untrained eye, and her finest operatives emerged from the shadows, equipped with precision and intent.

The conflict that ensued was a well-orchestrated ballet of strategy and counterattacks. Boss Chick's operatives unveiled their presence, surrounding Sister Mary with the surgical skill of seasoned predators. But Sister Mary was no unsuspecting prey. She had built her empire on anticipation, on expecting the knife hidden beneath the cloak of night.

The city's heartbeats were muffled under the looming threat of cartel rivalry. Sister Mary, known for her ambitious empire, found solace inside her vehicle, a fortress on wheels amidst the chaos of the world outside. Boss Chick, sensing a moment of vulnerability in her adversary, believed the time had come to confront and overturn the balance. Sister Mary reclined in the leather embrace of her SUV, the dashboard's glow a specter in the twilight. She knew the danger, Boss Chick's shadow had grown too long, spilling over the boundaries that had kept an uneasy peace.

Across the divide, Boss Chick observed from her own steel bastion, her gaze locked onto the silhouette of her rival. Tension knotted the air, a prelude to the imminent clash. The storm broke with a shiver of steel, a signal misunderstood, a boundary unwittingly crossed. The hush of the evening was shattered by the roar of engines as Boss Chick signaled her fleet. This was no hail of bullets, but a thunderous advance towards a line that Sister Mary had sworn to defend.

Caught within her sanctuary, Sister Mary felt the first wave, not of flesh but of spirit, wounds began to bleed as her world shook. With resolution clinched between her teeth, she slipped behind the wheel and turned the ignition. Her only thought was to reach sanctity of the law's embrace. Sister Mary bulldozed her way from the turf, the gravity of her situation clawing at her psyche. Boss Chick followed suit, her own Benz growling through the arteries of asphalt behind her. It wasn't the piercing pain of physical harm that drove them, but the sting of betrayal and the need to reclaim their dignity.

Sister Mary sped through the city onto the highway, leaving Boss Chick blocks away as Sister Mary disappeared into traffic. Sister Mary grabbed her phone and attempted to call Mustafa, but he failed to pick the phone up. not knowing that he had been killed by Boss Chick and Con. "Damn, this nigga Mustafa won't answer the phone," she screamed out loud as she continued to go over the speed limit on the highway.

"Con, this bitch got away again, as you can see. We have to catch her on a club night or with another bitch. Maybe Candice and Caressa can help us get this bitch for a nice price!"

"Yeah, you right. Them twins are money thirsty like Mustafa. A couple of thousand, them bitches will do anything. I believe I have their number somewhere in my phone. Let me check while we try to see where Sister Mary went to, baby!"

"This shit crazy, this bitch got little on us. Believe me, the next time it will go down and she will never have the chance to run like a little church house bitch. Feel me, Con?"

"Yeah, baby." He smiled.

Boss Chick stood in the warehouse with Con on the opposite side of a long, steel table. She looked down at the flawless, neatly wrapped bricks of cocaine that were laid out perfectly on the table.

Ain't this bitch nice?" Con asked, waving his hand over the shipment like a game show host showing a winning prize. "You can't beat getting this shit as easy as we did."

"You ain't never lied, nigga." Boss Chick, excitement apparent in her eyes but her face showed that she was cool about it. She was still kind of stunned that Con had pulled off the transport without even consulting her on a shipping method.

"Like Rambo promised, this is straight off that banana boat. Not one bit stepped on at all. Purest you'll ever get in the United States," Con told her, sticking his chest out proudly. He had something to prove to Boss Chick, and this shipment was just what he needed to make the point.

Boss Chick looked over at him and she felt funny deep inside... a tingle that he didn't get from many women. Con was as handsome as the first day Boss Chick laid eyes on him, but today, after what she'd accomplished, Con looked even more handsome to her. Boss Chick loved to see him in green, so the green blazer she wore with her perfect breasts peeking out was doing something to him. He remembered the hot night they met in Atlanta and wondered if Con ever thought about it like she did. Neither of them had ever mentioned it again and Con knew that for the past three months, Karla had been living with Boss Chick's grandfather and receiving frequent visits from Boss Chick. Con surprised that Boss Chick and Karla had taken things to the next level, so Con stepped back to protect her own heart.

"Why you staring at me like that? I got something on my face or body?" Con asked, snapping Boss Chick out of her daydream.

"Nah, nah, nah. Nothing like that. So, you... we need to get this out to the streets and see how it goes," Boss Chick told him, quickly changing the subject back to strictly business. She picked up a brick of the pure cocaine and held it for a few minutes. "This is good... real good."

"Gucci is a dead issue now, right?" Con came back quickly. Con had already kept a secret about information with Gucci.

"I'll handle Gucci, you handle distribution," Boss Chick said to Con. Boss Chick had already been dodging calls from Gucci for the past month, while she waited to see if Rambo would make good on his deal. Boss Chick finally got tired Gucci's incessant calls and changed her phone number. Boss Chick told herself she'd get in contact with Gucci later, in due time. Her plan was to make Gucci whole for the last shipment and then let Gucci down easily, with the hopes they could just part peacefully. It was a lofty goal and hope and Boss Chick knew it. She grabbed a duffle bag filled with guns and told Con, "Let's take it somewhere."

***

Sister Mary awoke to a loud crashing noise in her mansion on the west side of town. Not too many people knew about her new living arrangements, so she was immediately stricken with panic. Her mind was still a little fuzzy with sleep, but Sister Mary had enough clarity to grab for the small .380 caliber handgun she kept in her nightstand drawer. The noise came again, but this time Sister Mary was on her feet with her gun out in front of her. Her heart raced so fast she could barely breathe, but she was not going to lie down and let herself be an easy victim again.

Sister Mary slowly turned the doorknob on her bedroom door and just as she went to step through the doorway, she felt something pulling her forward.

Ahh!" Her scream was short lived as someone snatched her by her hair and dragged her down to the floor. Sister Mary tried to get her finger into the trigger of her gun, but a brute force punch to the face dizzied her so badly she completely lost her grip on her weapon.

"Help," she croaked out, but another slam to the face caused the words to tumble right back down her throat. Sister Mary could feel herself moving now, but not of her own will.

"Sit her in front of me," a female voice that she recognized demanded. Sister Mary was weak, but her attackers slammed her into one of her own chairs and pulled her head up so she met their boss.

"Boss Chick," Sister Mary stammered, her lips beginning to swell. She believed she knew her voice and her scent, Chanel perfume, anywhere.

"Caressa and Candice told me where your new mansion was. You a dead bitch now."

"What? I... I don't know what you're talking about," she groaned, her legs swinging in and out nervously. As far as Sister Mary knew, things between Mustafa and Boss Chick had worked out perfectly for years as she thought before he got killed.

"I guess Sister Mary really thinks she is the queen of the cartel?" Con asked. "I hear that's what she calls herself these days, Queen Mary."

Boss Chick shook her head from side to side. She hadn't heard or seen Sister Mary since she fled the scene of the battle that was about to go down in front of her mansion.

"What's up with your new supplier, Sister Mary?"

"Please. Let me call them," Sister Mary pleaded. barely able to speak through her swollen lips.

"No need to call them, bitch! I will send them a short message."

"No! No! Please, Boss Chick," Sister Mary screamed, bucking her body in the chair was beings restrained in. It didn't take long for them to silence her. "Fuck you," she whispered defiantly. She didn't care what they did to her. She would never give her plug up to get murdered.

"You wan' play hard, bitch?" Con punched Sister Mary across her face so hard that more blood and a tooth shot from her lips. Sister Mary was taking the hits like a pro boxer.

Each time they hit her she forced herself to raise her head to meet them face to face now. Her attackers didn't know that Sister Mary had been beaten all of her life, and it took much more to get her to fold on her cartel family.

Sister Mary was fighting, flailing her arms. They came loose from the chair. She was fighting so hard she didn't hear anything at the moment.

"Hit her again. Make her shit on herself," Con growled evilly. When Boss Chick moved in to hit Sister Mary, she extended her right arm and swiped at her, catching the end of Boss Chick long dreads. Sister Mary yanked wildly on Boss Chick's locks and was shocked when several of them came off of her head.

"This bitch crazy, Boss Chick!" He was so mad that he had been exposed that he punched Sister Mary her stomach, chest, like she was a man. The hits were so hard, her back teeth clicked together. Sister Mary made a loud noise, and her body folded as pain shot through her chest and stomach so fast and furious, she just knew her heart had exploded. Sister Mary's oxygen was just cut off, but before her world went black, she finally heard Mustafa calling her name frantically.

Mustafa! Mustafa!" Sister Mary was screaming inside of her clouded head, but she could not get the words out with the amount of pain wracking her body. Another hard blow made Sister Mary's eyes snap shut by themselves, and piss leaked from her bladder involuntarily.

"Somebody else here... Bitch!" Con asked.

"No! You hoes going pay for this just done to me!"

"Shut up, bitch!" Boss Chick barked and with her last blow to her head and a shot to the brain from Boss Chick's Glock .40, Sister Mary's world finally went completely black.

Lock Down Publications and Ca$h Presents
Assisted Publishing Packages

Due to an increase in the price of services we have increased our prices. The prices below reflect the price increase as of 11/1/24.

BASIC PACKAGE	UPGRADED PACKAGE
$699	$1000
Editing	Typing
Cover Design	Editing
Formatting	Cover Design
	Formatting
	Upload eBooks to Amazon
	Upload Paperback to Amazon
ADVANCE PACKAGE	LDP SUPREME PACKAGE
$1,400	$1,700
Typing	Typing
Editing (line editing/content)	Editing (line editing/content)
Cover Design	Cover Design
Formatting	Formatting
Copyright Registration	Copyright Registration
Proofreading	Proofreading
Upload eBooks to Amazon	Set up Amazon Account
Upload Paperback to Amazon	Upload eBooks to Amazon
	Upload Paperback to Amazon
	Advertise on LDP's Amazon and Facebook Page

***

Other services available upon request.
Additional charges may apply

Lock Down Publications
P.O. Box 944
Stockbridge, GA 30281-9998
Phone: 470 303-9761
Email: lockdownpublications@gmail.com

Submission Guideline

Submit the first three chapters of your completed manuscript to ldpsubmissions@gmail.com. In the subject line add **Your Book's Title**. The manuscript must be in a Word Doc file and sent as an attachment. Document should be in Times New Roman, double spaced, and in size 12 font. Also, provide your synopsis and full contact information. If sending multiple submissions, they must each be in a separate email.

Have a story but no way to send it electronically? You can still submit to LDP/Ca$h Presents. Send in the first three chapters, written or typed, of your completed manuscript to:

LDP: Submissions Dept
P.O. Box 944
Stockbridge, GA 30281-9998

DO NOT send original manuscript. Must be a duplicate. Provide your synopsis and a cover letter containing your full contact information.

Thanks for considering LDP and Ca$h Presents.

NEW RELEASES

BLOODLINE OF A SAVAGE 1-3
THESE VICIOUS STREETS 1-3
RELENTLESS GOON 1-3
BY PRINCE A. TAUHID

THE BUTTERFLY MAFIA 1-3
BY FUMIYA PAYNE

A THUG'S STREET PRINCESS 1&2
BY MEESHA

CITY OF SMOKE 3
BY MOLOTTI

GET IT IN SLUGS 1 &2
BY B. STALL

STANDING ON HER BUSINESS 1&2
BY DG SANTANA

STEPPERS 1,2&3
THE REAL BADDIES OF CHI-RAQ
BY KING RIO

THE LANE 1&2
BY KEN-KEN SPENCE

THUG OF SPADES 1&2
LOVE IN THE TRENCHES 2
CORNER BOYS
BY COREY ROBINSON

TIL DEATH 3
BY ARYANNA

THE BIRTH OF A GANGSTER 4
BY DELMONT PLAYER

PRODUCT OF THE STREETS 1-3
BY DEMOND "MONEY" ANDERSON

NO TIME FOR ERROR
BY KEESE

MONEY HUNGRY DEMONS 1-2
BY TRANAY ADAMS

HUB CITY MENACE 1-3
BY J. WHITE

A THUGGISH PASSION 1&2
LAND OF DA HOOLIGANZ 1-4
KILLAZ ON STANDBY 1&2
BY IRA B.

FO'EVA ROLLIN 1&2
BY ASSA RAYMOND BAKER

THE LEVEL UP 1&3
BY LUXURY KING

Coming Soon from Lock Down Publications/Ca$h Presents

IF YOU CROSS ME ONCE 6
ANGEL V
By Anthony Fields

A THUGS STREET PRINCESS 3
By Meesha

CORNER BOYS 2
By Corey Robinson

THA TAKEOVER
By Keith Chandler

BETRAYAL OF A G 2
By Ray Vinci

SAVAGE FAMILY EMPIRE 1&2
SOULLESS GOON 1,2&3
THE DIRTY SIDE OF MONEY 1,2&3
By Prince

FOR MY ENEMY'S SAKE
AMBITIONS OF A SLIDER
FRESH OFF DA PORCH
By IRA B.

THE TRUCKLOAD 1-4
TIPPIN' THE SCALES 1-3
BAD BITCHES WIT GUNZ 3
PROBLEM SOLVED 2
By Christopher "Diesel" Hornezes

Available Now

RESTRAINING ORDER 1 & 2
By **CA$H & Coffee**

LOVE KNOWS NO BOUNDARIES 1-3
By **Coffee**

RAISED AS A GOON I, II, III & IV
BRED BY THE SLUMS I, II, III
BLAST FOR ME I & II
ROTTEN TO THE CORE I II III
A BRONX TALE I, II, III
DUFFLE BAG CARTEL I II III IV V VI
HEARTLESS GOON I II III IV V
A SAVAGE DOPEBOY I II
DRUG LORDS I II III
CUTTHROAT MAFIA I II
KING OF THE TRENCHES
By **Ghost**

LAY IT DOWN I & II
LAST OF A DYING BREED I II
BLOOD STAINS OF A SHOTTA I & II III
By **Jamaica**

LOYAL TO THE GAME I II III
LIFE OF SIN I, II III
By **TJ & Jelissa**

IF LOVING HIM IS WRONG…I & II
LOVE ME EVEN WHEN IT HURTS I II III
By **Jelissa**

PUSH IT TO THE LIMIT
By **Bre' Hayes**

BLOODY COMMAS I & II
SKI MASK CARTEL I, II & III
KING OF NEW YORK I II, III IV V
RISE TO POWER I II III
COKE KINGS I II III IV V
BORN HEARTLESS I II III IV
KING OF THE TRAP I II
By **T.J. Edwards**

WHEN THE STREETS CLAP BACK I & II III
THE HEART OF A SAVAGE I II III IV
MONEY MAFIA I II
LOYAL TO THE SOIL I II III
By **Jibril Williams**

A DISTINGUISHED THUG STOLE MY HEART I II & III
LOVE SHOULDN'T HURT I II III IV
RENEGADE BOYS 1-4
PAID IN KARMA 1-3
SAVAGE STORMS 1-3
AN UNFORESEEN LOVE 1-3
BABY, I'M WINTERTIME COLD 1-3
A THUG'S STREET PRINCESS 1&2
By **Meesha**

A GANGSTER'S CODE 1-3
A GANGSTER'S SYN 1-3
THE SAVAGE LIFE 1-3
CHAINED TO THE STREETS 1-3
BLOOD ON THE MONEY 1-3
A GANGSTA'S PAIN 1-3
BEAUTIFUL LIES AND UGLY TRUTHS
CHURCH IN THESE STREETS
By **J-Blunt**

CUM FOR ME 1-8
An LDP Erotica Collaboration

BLOOD OF A BOSS 1-5
SHADOWS OF THE GAME
TRAP BASTARD
By **Askari**

THE STREETS BLEED MURDER 1-3
THE HEART OF A GANGSTA 1-3
By **Jerry Jackson**

WHEN A GOOD GIRL GOES BAD
By **Adrienne**

THE COST OF LOYALTY 1-3
By **Kweli**

BRIDE OF A HUSTLA 1-3
THE FETTI GIRLS 1-3
CORRUPTED BY A GANGSTA 1-4
BLINDED BY HIS LOVE
THE PRICE YOU PAY FOR LOVE 1-3
DOPE GIRL MAGIC 1-3
By **Destiny Skai**

A KINGPIN'S AMBITION
A KINGPIN'S AMBITION II
I MURDER FOR THE DOUGH
By **Ambitious**

TRUE SAVAGE 1-7
DOPE BOY MAGIC 1-3
MIDNIGHT CARTEL 1-3
CITY OF KINGZ 1&2
NIGHTMARE ON SILENT AVE
THE PLUG OF LIL MEXICO 1&2
CLASSIC CITY
By **Chris Green**

A GANGSTER'S REVENGE 1-4
THE BOSS MAN'S DAUGHTERS 1-5
A SAVAGE LOVE 1&2
BAE BELONGS TO ME 1&2
A HUSTLER'S DECEIT 1-3
WHAT BAD BITCHES DO 1-3
SOUL OF A MONSTER 1-3
KILL ZONE
A DOPE BOY'S QUEEN 1-3
TIL DEATH 1-3
IMMA DIE BOUT MINE 1-6
DYING FOR LIKES
By **Aryanna**

A DOPEBOY'S PRAYER
By **Eddie "Wolf" Lee**

THE KING CARTEL 1-3
By **Frank Gresham**

THESE NIGGAS AIN'T LOYAL 1-3
By **Nikki Tee**

GANGSTA SHYT 1-3
By **CATO**

THE ULTIMATE BETRAYAL
By **Phoenix**

BOSS'N UP 1-3
By **Royal Nicole**

I LOVE YOU TO DEATH
By **Destiny J**

I RIDE FOR MY HITTA
I STILL RIDE FOR MY HITTA
By **Misty Holt**

LOVE & CHASIN' PAPER
By **Qay Crockett**

TO DIE IN VAIN
SINS OF A HUSTLA
By **ASAD**

BROOKLYN HUSTLAZ
By **Boogsy Morina**

BROOKLYN ON LOCK 1 & 2
By **Sonovia**

GANGSTA CITY
By **Teddy Duke**

A DRUG KING AND HIS DIAMOND 1-3
A DOPEMAN'S RICHES
HER MAN, MINE'S TOO 1&2
CASH MONEY HO'S
THE WIFEY I USED TO BE 1&2
PRETTY GIRLS DO NASTY THINGS
By **Nicole Goosby**

LIPSTICK KILLAH 1-3
CRIME OF PASSION 1-3
FRIEND OR FOE 1-3
By **Mimi**

TRAPHOUSE KING 1-3
KINGPIN KILLAZ 1-3
STREET KINGS 1&2
PAID IN BLOOD 1&2
CARTEL KILLAZ 1-3
DOPE GODS 1&2
By **Hood Rich**

THE STREETS ARE CALLING
By **Duquie Wilson**

STEADY MOBBN' 1-3
THE STREETS STAINED MY SOUL 1-3
By **Marcellus Allen**

WHO SHOT YA 1-3
SON OF A DOPE FIEND 1-4
HEAVEN GOT A GHETTO 1&2
SKI MASK MONEY 1&2
By **Renta**

GORILLAZ IN THE BAY 1-4
TEARS OF A GANGSTA 1/&2
3X KRAZY 1&2
STRAIGHT BEAST MODE 1&2
By **DE'KARI**

TRIGGADALE 1-3
MURDA WAS THE CASE 1-3
By **Elijah R. Freeman**

SLAUGHTER GANG 1-3
RUTHLESS HEART 1-3
By **Willie Slaughter**

GOD BLESS THE TRAPPERS 1-3
THESE SCANDALOUS STREETS 1-3
FEAR MY GANGSTA 1-5
THESE STREETS DON'T LOVE NOBODY 1-2
BURY ME A G 1-5
A GANGSTA'S EMPIRE 1-4
THE DOPEMAN'S BODYGAURD 1&2
THE REALEST KILLAZ 1-3
THE LAST OF THE OGS 1-3
By **Tranay Adams**

MARRIED TO A BOSS 1-3
By **Destiny Skai & Chris Green**

KINGZ OF THE GAME 1-7
CRIME BOSS 1-4
By **Playa Ray**

FUK SHYT
By **Blakk Diamond**

DON'T F#CK WITH MY HEART 1&2
By **Linnea**

ADDICTED TO THE DRAMA 1-3
IN THE ARM OF HIS BOSS
By **Jamila**

LOYALTY AIN'T PROMISED 1&2
By **Keith Williams**

YAYO 1-4
A SHOOTER'S AMBITION 1&2
BRED IN THE GAME
By **S. Allen**

TRAP GOD 1-3
RICH $AVAGE 1-3
MONEY IN THE GRAVE 1-3
CARTEL MONEY 1&2
By **Martell Troublesome Bolden**

FOREVER GANGSTA 1&2
GLOCKS ON SATIN SHEETS 1&2
By **Adrian Dulan**

TOE TAGZ 1-4
LEVELS TO THIS SHYT 1&2
IT'S JUST ME AND YOU
By **Ah'Million**

KINGPIN DREAMS 1-3
RAN OFF ON DA PLUG
By **Paper Boi Rari**

THE STREETS MADE ME 1-3
By **Larry D. Wright**

CONFESSIONS OF A GANGSTA 1-4
CONFESSIONS OF A JACKBOY 1-3
CONFESSIONS OF A HITMAN
CONFESSIONS OF A DOPE BOY
By **Nicholas Lock**

I'M NOTHING WITHOUT HIS LOVE
SINS OF A THUG
TO THE THUG I LOVED BEFORE
A GANGSTA SAVED XMAS
IN A HUSTLER I TRUST
By **Monet Dragun**

QUIET MONEY 1-3
THUG LIFE 1-3
EXTENDED CLIP 1&2
A GANGSTA'S PARADISE
By **Trai'Quan**

CAUGHT UP IN THE LIFE 1-3
THE STREETS NEVER LET GO 1-3
By **Robert Baptiste**

NEW TO THE GAME 1-3
MONEY, MURDER & MEMORIES 1-3
By **Malik D. Rice**

CREAM 2-3
THE STREETS WILL TALK
By **Yolanda Moore**

THE STREETS WILL NEVER CLOSE 1-3
By **K'ajji**

LIFE OF A SAVAGE 1-4
A GANGSTA'S QUR'AN 1-4
MURDA SEASON 1-3
GANGLAND CARTEL 1-3
CHI'RAQ GANGSTAS 1-4
KILLERS ON ELM STREET 1-3
JACK BOYZ N DA BRONX 1-3
A DOPEBOY'S DREAM 1-3
JACK BOYS VS DOPE BOYS 1-3
COKE GIRLZ
COKE BOYS
SOSA GANG 1&2
BRONX SAVAGES
BODYMORE KINGPINS
BLOOD OF A GOON
By **Romell Tukes**

CONCRETE KILLA 1-3
VICIOUS LOYALTY 1-3
BLOODY MONEY BAGS
By **Kingpen**

THE ULTIMATE SACRIFICE 1-6
KHADIFI
IF YOU CROSS ME ONCE 1-3
ANGEL 1-4
IN THE BLINK OF AN EYE
By **Anthony Fields**

THE LIFE OF A HOOD STAR
By **Ca$h & Rashia Wilson**

NIGHTMARES OF A HUSTLA 1-3
BLOOD AND GAMES 1&2
By **King Dream**

GHOST MOB
By **Stilloan Robinson**

HARD AND RUTHLESS 1&2
MOB TOWN 251
THE BILLIONAIRE BENTLEYS 1-3
REAL G'S MOVE IN SILENCE
By **Von Diesel**

MOB TIES 1-7
SOUL OF A HUSTLER, HEART OF A KILLER 1-3
GORILLAZ IN THE TRENCHES
OOPS CRY TOO 1&2
THE DAUGHTER OF A CARTEL BOSS
By **SayNoMore**

BODYMORE MURDERLAND 1-3
THE BIRTH OF A GANGSTER 1-4
By **Delmont Player**

FOR THE LOVE OF A BOSS 1&2
By **C. D. Blue**

KILLA KOUNTY 1-5
TENDER
By **Khufu**

MOBBED UP 1-4
THE BRICK MAN 1-5
THE COCAINE PRINCESS 1-10
STEPPERS 1-3
SUPER GREMLIN 1-4
A GANGSTA'S SON
By **King Rio**

MONEY GAME 1&2
By **Smoove Dolla**

A GANGSTA'S KARMA 1-5
By **FLAME**

KING OF THE TRENCHES 1-3
By **GHOST & TRANAY ADAMS**

BAD BITCHES WIT GUNZ 1&2
PROBLEM SOLVED
By **"Christopher Diesel" Hornezes**

QUEEN OF THE ZOO 1&2
By **Black Migo**

GRIMEY WAYS 1-3
BETRAYAL OF A G
By **Ray Vinci**

XMAS WITH AN ATL SHOOTER
By **Ca$h & Destiny Skai**

KING KILLA 1&2
By **Vincent "Vitto" Holloway**

BETRAYAL OF A THUG 1&2
By **Fre$h**

COUNTDOWN OF A KILLA 1&2
SEX, MURDER AND GOD 1&2
GUNS DOWN, BOTTOMS UP 1&2
By Lo-Life

THE MURDER QUEENS 1-7
By **Michael Gallon**

FOR THE LOVE OF BLOOD 1-4
By **Jamel Mitchell**

HOOD CONSIGLIERE 1&2
NO TIME FOR ERROR
By **Keese**

PROTÉGÉ OF A LEGEND 1,2&3
LOVE IN THE TRENCHES 1&2
By **Corey Robinson**

THE PLUG'S RUTHLESS DAUGHTER 1&2
By **Tony Daniels**

BORN IN THE GRAVE 1-3
CRIME PAYS
By **Self Made Tay**

MOAN IN MY MOUTH
By **XTASY**

TORN BETWEEN A GANGSTER AND A GENTLEMAN
By **J-BLUNT & Miss Kim**

LOYALTY IS EVERYTHING 1-3
CITY OF SMOKE 1-3
By **Molotti**

HERE TODAY GONE TOMORROW 1&2
By **Fly Rock**

WOMEN LIE MEN LIE 1-4
FIFTY SHADES OF SNOW 1-3
STACK BEFORE YOU SPLURGE
GIRLS FALL LIKE DOMINOES
NAÏVE TO THE STREETS
By **ROY MILLIGAN**

PILLOW PRINCESS
By **S. Hawkins**

THE BUTTERFLY MAFIA 1-3
SALUTE MY SAVAGERY 1&2
By **Fumiya Payne**

THE LANE 1&2
By Ken-Ken Spence

THE PUSSY TRAP 1-5
By **Nene Capri**

DIRTY DNA
By **Blaque**

SANCTIFIED AND HORNY
by **XTASY**

BOOKS BY LDP'S CEO, CA$H

TRUST IN NO MAN
TRUST IN NO MAN 2
TRUST IN NO MAN 3
BONDED BY BLOOD
SHORTY GOT A THUG
THUGS CRY
THUGS CRY 2
THUGS CRY 3
TRUST NO BITCH
TRUST NO BITCH 2
TRUST NO BITCH 3
TIL MY CASKET DROPS
RESTRAINING ORDER
RESTRAINING ORDER 2
IN LOVE WITH A CONVICT
LIFE OF A HOOD STAR
XMAS WITH AN ATL SHOOTER

www.ingramcontent.com/pod-product-compliance
Lightning Source LLC
Chambersburg PA
CBHW071220260626
47162CB00004B/1370